Bein' Dead Ain't No Excuse

by

Penny Burwell Ewing

The Haunted Salon Series, Book 4

Bein' Dead Ain't No Excuse

COPYRIGHT © 2018 by Penny Burwell Ewing

Cover Art by *Debbie Taylor*

The Wild Rose Press, Inc.
PO Box 708
Adams Basin, NY 14410-0708
Visit us at www.thewildrosepress.com

Publishing History
First Fantasy Rose Edition, 2018
Print ISBN 978-1-5092-2278-0
Digital ISBN 978-1-5092-2279-7

The Haunted Salon Series, Book 4
Published in the United States of America

I snapped out of my paralysis at the sight of two, bulb-eyed *things* barreling toward me, their dark wings whirring and strings of yellow sulfurous ribbons pouring from their open, snarling mouths. Profanity filled the cool autumn night with spews of hatred and damnation for the heavenly as one of the beasts clashed with Scarlett in mid-air.

"Holy crap," I screamed in a blind panic and drew my sword and scrambled off the branch to meet the incoming missile speeding toward me. With both hands clasped on the hilt of the sword I could hardly maintain flight, and I dipped close to the ground and did a back flip as the bat-like thing took a swing at me with his fiery sword. It grazed my ankle, and a burning sting set my flesh on fire. Wounded, I hit the ground and rolled over on my back. Our swords met and clashed. Sparks flew in every direction as again and again our swords met.

"Get on your feet!" I heard Scarlett yell somewhere above me. "He has the advantage."

Screaming with fear and frustration, I tried to recall the basics of sword fighting taught by the archangel Hazell, but my mind grew hazy as the enemy's sword pricked my upper arm. Pain blazed through me, and I barely parried the next jab. From my position on the ground I watched his fiery sword arch upwards, and I knew I was done for. I closed my eyes and said a quick prayer.

Dedication

To my parents, Bruce and Alice Burwell, and my stepfather, James W. Joiner. Thank you for your unending support of my writing pursuits. You've propped me up in down times and never stopped believing in me. I'm where I am because of you.

Also, to the memory of James and Juanita Ewing, who inspired the loving characters of Harland and Annie Mae Tucker, and the farm where Jolene and her two sisters grew into strong, independent women of courage and unwavering love of family.

Cast of Characters

Jolene Claiborne – Heaven saves its best punch for last, but this spunky Southern belle is up for the challenge. Or is she headed straight for the devil's domain and an ending she never imagined?

Deena Sinclair – Somebody's going to die if they screw up her wedding plans.

Billie Jo Hazard – She's carrying a special package.

Roddy Hazard – He's never had a wandering eye until now.

Annie Mae Tucker – When your number's up, better get packing.

Harland Tucker – He's had enough digging for peanuts in the dirt. Wanderlust has him by the boot strings.

Samuel Bradford – Whiskey Creek's finest hung up his badge for snow-capped mountains in the Wild West. But there's no gold in them hills for a single man.

Dr. Preston Neally – He's out to carve his initials in Jolene's heart.

Diane Downey – The Golden Rule doesn't apply to her.

Sonya Jones – There's more to this songbird than just a pretty voice.

Jimbo White – Thou shalt not covet thy neighbor's peanut farm.

Lilith Lacewell – Beauty is in the eye of the beholder. This gorgeous redhead has a plan to steal more than hearts and husbands.

Madame Mia – The beautiful psychic may have just met her biggest challenge yet.

Scarlett Cantrell – Being booted out of heaven is the worst fate for this wayward soul who is trying to earn her wings.

Saint Peter – Heaven's gatekeeper is threatening to lock

the Pearly Gates against a certain sassy Southern belle who doesn't play by the rules.

Chapter One
The List

Picking a fight with Heaven isn't for the faint of heart, or even for the strongest one. It's reserved for the stupid, like me. Only a pig-headed Southerner would lift her fist to the sky and challenge the Master of the Universe to a duel of wills. But that's what I did when Mama's name landed on Heaven's list of arriving saints.

Scarlett Cantrell, that's my gal-pal from the Other Side, alerted me of Mama's impending departure on the long, black train. Well, that doesn't fit into my plans at all. I have two beaus fighting over me, Deena's wedding is less than two weeks away, and Billie Jo's expecting a baby in the spring. How can we Tucker gals get along without our mama? Well, we can't. That's why I'm speeding toward the farm—to prevent Heaven from playing target practice with Mama.

I arrived at the farm in a cloud of red dust and bolted from the car for the back kitchen door in pursuit of my sainted parents. Rushing through the unlocked door, I found an empty kitchen, much to my disappointment.

"Mama?" I called out. No response. "Daddy?" No answer from the empty house. Retracing my steps, I checked the garage for their cars. Check. They were here somewhere on the farm. Half out of my mind with worry, I sprinted for the barn and heard the murmur of angry voices as I drew near the opened doors.

"Now you listen to me, Annie Mae Tucker," my father's stern voice rose above the clucking chickens and shuffling hooves. "We're selling the farm and moving to Florida."

"And I say different." Mama's voice was pitched high. "We've got a new grandbaby on the way. I'm staying put."

"And I'm selling the farm and moving to Florida, old woman."

"Over my dead body, asshole. This is my home, and you can't sell it without my signature. What are you doing? Let go! Stop, Harland!"

With those angry words spilling out into the frosty morning, I scrambled through the open doors to witness my parents tussling on the upper hayloft. I hesitated, my mind not entirely processing the scene unfolding before me. Before I could open my mouth to protest, Mama let out a scream and pitched forward off the loft and landed with a soft thump on the hay piled below.

The scream on my lips burst out, and I rushed to her side and bent over her still figure. My hands were shaking as I brushed the dried grass from her pale face. "Mama?" I patted her face. "Can you hear me?" From the loft above, I could hear Daddy's frantic cries while he scrambled down the wooden ladder.

"Land sakes, Annie Mae!" he bellowed, as he sank down beside me. His hands were shaking like mine when he lifted Mama's limp hand. "You trying to kill yourself?"

At his words, I shot him an angry look. "You pushed her," I accused. "I saw and heard the whole

2

thing."

Daddy blanched and pulled back in surprise, but before he could respond to my hurtful words, Mama moaned and then opened her eyes. "I'm fine, just winded." She smiled up at Daddy. "Harland, help me up."

Together, we stood Mama on her feet. "Are you sure you're okay?" I asked as I plucked strands of hay from her short, graying blonde hair. "I believe you should be checked out at the emergency room. That was a nasty fall."

"Nonsense," she huffed. "Just a minor accident." She brushed hay from her worn jeans. "I slipped and fell, that's all."

"Minor accident?" I closed my eyes and blew out a breath. "Premeditated is more like it."

Daddy gave a noticeable sigh. "Now, Jolene, don't be silly. I didn't push your mama. I grabbed her when she slipped. I tried to *prevent* her fall."

Scarlett's warning rang in my ears, and I ditched the rest of my common sense. "I see it differently." I plunged ahead hotly, "with her dead, you can sell the farm and disappear with all the proceeds. Disappearing *is* your specialty."

Mama pinched me hard on the upper arm. "Leave the past be, Jolene. We paid for our mistakes a hundred times over, and we'll not apologize again." She linked her arm in Daddy's. "Now apologize to your father."

The words stuck to the roof of my mouth as the full impact of my accusation hit me. Heat flooded my face while I continued to stare in mute silence at my father, who seemed to wither in height with each passing second. His once proud face, wrinkled heavily, highlighted the downward turn of his mouth, and his eyes shifted away when I tried to capture them with mine.

Once again, my impetuousness had reaped immense damage. As usual, I hadn't stopped to weigh the consequences of my rash actions. Words once spoken are hard to take back. Especially when you've just accused your father of attempted murder.

"We're waiting, Jolene," Mama's snide voice cut into my thoughts. "And why aren't you at work? The salon is short-staffed with Billie Jo out. Deena's nerves are frazzled with wedding preparations, and here you are provoking hard feelings with your razor-sharp tongue."

Daddy put an arm around my shoulders. "Leave her be, Annie Mae." His voice softened, "Tell me what's got you jumping at shadows, honey."

I slipped my arm around his waist. "I'm sorry, Daddy. If I'd taken the time to think things through....I misjudged you..." My words choked on a sob. "But Mama's in trouble."

He steered me out of the barn. "Let's go up to the house. Annie Mae can whip up a quick breakfast, and you can tell us what's got you so frazzled."

Mama kept silent as we climbed the back porch steps and entered the warm, cozy kitchen. She headed straight for the refrigerator and pulled out a slab of thick-cut bacon, and her pursed lips never cracked a smile. As she set about frying the bacon, Daddy poured us both a cup of strong, black coffee and joined me at the table.

He squeezed my hand. "Okay, honey, tell us what's on your mind. Whatever's going on, we'll handle it as a family."

Okay, the time had come, but as I sat there staring into Daddy's gentle brown eyes, I choked. How do you tell your mama that her neck is on Heaven's chopping block? The words stuck in my throat and my head pounded from trying to make sense of an impossible situation. I couldn't find the right words or a gentle way to break the news, so I just opened my mouth and released the bomb.

Mama dropped her fork, it hit the stove, and then crashed to the floor. Daddy bolted up from his chair at the table and walked out the kitchen door without a backward glance. And me—I was left running full speed toward disaster without the brakes on.

****

"Are you out of your mind?" Deena's shrill voice blasted over the rock-n-roll tune streaming over the salon's speakers. Of course, several heads swung in our direction with avid curiosity streaming from their gleaming eyes.

I grabbed my sister's arm and propelled her past the flower garden in the reception area and into her office. "Damn, Deena, give me a break, will ya? Every vulture in Whiskey Creek is out for new gossip."

Deena snatched her arm out of my grip. "Give you a break? Ha! You're the one who peeled out of here this morning and left me here to deal with *your*," and here she paused for emphasis, "boyfriends." She waved two fingers under my nose. "Not one, mind you, but two. Why can't you settle for one man like the rest of us, Jolene?" Her voice rose. "And those damn flowers are giving me a headache."

The flower garden was a result of clashing

testosterone and the almighty male ego. It had started with Preston Neally's autumn bouquet and ended with Bradford's insane attempt to woo me away from the young doctor. And now Deena's office and reception area were filled with floral arrangements of every size, shape, and color. Oh, boy, what a story, and better told elsewhere because I'm running out of time.

"I'm sorry, but I had an emergency. A life and death emergency." I tried to touch her, but she moved away with her face pulled into a frown.

"Another cockamamie ghost thingy," she blurted and spun around to face me, her eyes spitting fire. "We're short-staffed with Billie Jo out on maternity leave, Holly gave her two-week notice, my wedding is ten days away, and we're closed up in my office discussing another one of your *situations* instead of my nuptials. It's always about you, Jolene, and I'm sick of it. And your brash actions have injured two great guys. I hope they both dump you."

We stared at one another for several seconds, and seeing all the hurt and anger in Deena's eyes, I knew the time had come for me to lay it all out on the line. On hearing Mama's dilemma, Deena would probably stroke out and blame me, but I needed her help. Billie Jo's too. Mama's life was more important than her wedding, or Preston and Bradford's delicate feelings. To hell with them, and anyone else who got in my way.

Being the big sister, and tired of her silly tirade, I grabbed her upper arm and propelled her to her desk chair. "Sit down and shut up." I applied my superior weight, and she collapsed into the chair. "Maybe you didn't hear me when I said that Mama's number's up."

Deena's upper lip curled in a contemptuous twist.

"Get real, Jolene. I'm tired and stressed out this morning, and fed up with the drama. Really, Mama's number's up? What nonsense. And what does that mean, 'her number's up'?" Her eyes sparked rebellious fire at me.

I pondered for a moment of just whipping her ass like I used to do growing up but I stifled the impulse. Now I just plain felt sorry for her and didn't have the heart to mess up her face right before her big day. However, my patience can only stand so much without breaking down altogether, and I was close to losing it. The earlier scene at the farm had zapped my usually calm demeanor, and I had no way of knowing when the Death Angel would swoop down and murder Mama.

"Deena, honey," I patted her cheek with the tip of my finger. "Mama's on *The List*."

"What list?"

I rolled my eyes heavenward. "Good Lord, Deena. The list! The list! Haven't you been listening?" I clenched my hands to my side to keep from strangling her.

Confusion clouded her face. "I don't recall you mentioning a list."

I inhaled a deep breath, held it, and then exhaled at the count of ten. "When I met you at the back door, I told you about it then."

"Aren't you going to ask me about Sam and Preston?"

Dingbat! "What about them? They're gone. End of story."

Although my voice didn't betray my doubts, inside, my heart hammered against my chest as adrenaline pumped through my veins like a gasoline pipeline. I had dashed out of here so fast this morning that I had been unable to name the victor—because I had made a choice.

My choice. I could chuckle about it now. Dating two men had come down to this. Choose one, everyone demanded, so I did, but the chance to reward the winner never happened. Because of Scarlett and that damn list.

My choice?

Dr. Preston Neally.

Why you ask? Simple. No love involved. No chains of commitment. No dive off Heartbreak Ridge into a sea of self-pity. No tears, no pouting. No bogus claims of undying love. No Bridezilla. No bouquets to throw. No church to book. No disappointments. No divorce lawyers nipping at my heels. Just good old fashioned sex and companionship without the hassle of commitment.

And best of all, I could keep him at bay. Satisfy him with the crumbs of my affection. I'd learned to do that after Kenny and I divorced long ago. I had also learned that love rarely endures the test of time. Its faded glory had left a permanent scar on my heart. Only one man had since dared to enter that sacred place, and he had betrayed me.

Former Whiskey Creek police detective Samuel Bradford. Now, at this moment, driving into his future and leaving me behind. He had turned a deaf ear when I told him I could never leave my family and business here in Georgia for the snow-capped mountains of Wyoming.

He had made his choice, and I mine. Our paths dissected at the crossroads of life, and I couldn't have been any happier to have dodged the matrimonial bullet.

Deena's hand on my arm snapped me out of my musings. "Hey, I'm sorry for pitching a hissy fit. My nerves are strung out, and I'm ready to explode. But I'll try to listen and understand. Tell me about this list you claim Mama is on."

I glanced at my watch. "Holy crap. I forgot about my clients this morning. Damn, I'm losing my freakin' mind." My mood zapped, I sank down onto one of the chairs flanking her desk and released a great sigh of frustration.

"Taken care of. Holly switched them over to Lizzie, and she's glad for the extra money, so don't give it another thought. We have all the time you need," Deena assured me.

A brief tap sounded at the door before it sprung open to admit Billie Jo. "Mama called, so I came right over." She closed the door behind her and moved over to the vacant chair beside me. "She's really pissed at you, Jolene. Daddy too. I think you need to explain yourself."

I felt the tingle of her direct and examining stare and gauged how to open this conversation. At Billie Jo's age, late thirties, the doctor feared a possible miscarriage, so he had ordered her to rest until the birth of their baby. My brother-in-law, Roddy, would literally kill me if she lost their second child because of my recklessness. Caution was the keyword here.

"Are you sure you're up for this, Billie Jo?" My gaze roamed over her still flat stomach. "I don't want to further upset you and endanger the baby."

Billie Jo's serious expression softened. "Just give it to us straight. Everyone is overreacting with this pregnancy. I'm stronger than everyone thinks, including the doctor. I don't need to be on bed rest."

Deena gave a nod of agreement, so I began, "This morning I had an unexpected visit from Scarlett." Deena groaned, but I ignored her. "She returned to warn me that Mama's on the list of arriving saints."

"List of arriving saints?" Billie Jo questioned. "You lost me."

"This is the list you were referring to earlier?" Deena also spoke up.

I nodded. "Yes. I learned about the list only recently. I won't launch into that now, but believe me, there's a list in Heaven of arriving souls. Each soul is tried on their merits and then sent to the appropriate destination."

"That's not what we learned in Sunday school," Billie Jo observed. "So it's all about karma after all?"

"And you're trying to tell us that Mama's going to die?" Deena's voice and face mirrored disbelief. "Why that's crazy. No one knows these things."

I understood her confusion. Humans are not supposed to know the day or hour of our death, but I had an inside ear. Scarlett Cantrell—my personal angel with the personality of an aging beauty queen. Our love/hate relationship bordered on insane. Her death in my beauty shop was the beginning of my advent into the spirit world. But I don't consider myself a medium or a psychic. I see myself more of a spirit consultant to transient specters looking for human help. In the years since I discovered my talent, I've grown into a reasonably decent ghost detective. However, this newest adventure may prove to be my undoing. Scarlett warned of dire consequences if I interfered with

Heaven's plans, but I couldn't accept my mother's fate. Hence, this impromptu meeting with my sisters.

"You're forgetting Scarlett," I said. "She's my eyes and ears up there, and when she talks, I listen."

Billie Jo stood to her feet and walked over to gaze out the window where the sunlight beamed through. "Any idea when this is supposed to happen? Or how?"

"You don't believe this nonsense, do you, Billie Jo?" Deena jumped to her feet and raced around her desk. She plowed to a stop beside my chair.

"Yes, I do," she said with her back to us. "Jolene wouldn't make this up." Billie Jo turned to face us, her petite silhouette outlined by the streaming rays. "Would you, sis?"

I shook my head. "I would never lie to either one of you about a matter as serious as this. What I'm telling you is the truth. Mama's going to die if we don't stop it."

Deena expelled a heavy sigh. "I don't believe of word of it, but hypothetically, if I did, how do you propose we do that?"

My heart smiled at her choice of words. Gruff Deena always came around. "I don't know. Any suggestions?"

"Well, we can't hire a twenty-four-hour bodyguard, can we?" Deena smiled with encouragement. "Daddy wouldn't like a handsome stranger hanging around Mama. You know how jealous he is."

"What if we all take turns watching over her," Billie Jo suggested. "Between the family members, we should be able to keep her safe. Lynette is spending the night with her and Daddy, and can call me if there's any problem."

"Mama's not going to like all the attention," Deena said. "But I have an idea."

"What?" I prompted. "Anything will help."

"Well, Holly gave her two-week notice this morning. She's moving to Alabama to get married, and we're going to need a receptionist."

Billie Jo joined us at the desk. "And Mama's the perfect replacement."

I beamed at both of my sisters. "Brilliant. By hiring Mama, she's right under our noses all day. Daddy can take guard duty at night. With Deena's wedding closing in, one of us will always be with her. And since I'm single, I can spend most of my free time anchored at her side. If we're all agreed, then Deena, get Mama on the phone and see if she would like a job at Dixieland Salon."

Chapter Two
I Walk the Line

With the meeting behind me and some free time before my next client, I set about removing the floral arrangements from the reception area as a few of our patrons had complained about the overwhelmingly sweet scent contributing to their sinus miseries. Leaving one of the smaller bouquets on the reception desk, I decided to store the rest in the facial room until lunch at which time I would take the remainder over to the nursing home for the elderly to enjoy.

After retrieving the key from Deena's office, I approached the facial room door with anxious thoughts of the unwanted guest occupying the empty space. Unlocking the door, I pushed it open, stepped inside, and switched on the overhead light. Silence met my intrusion. From my position by the door, I could make a hasty retreat if the invisible force turned nasty. Except nothing happened. Nada. I took another step. And then another. Nothing. No bad vibrations at all.

Gaining courage, I backed out of the room and returned with several more bouquets in hand, and placed them on the table against the wall. With two more trips, I filled the room with floral arrangements from the reception area.

I had just set down the last vase when I heard the door click behind me—shutting out the sounds from the salon. A still silence came over the room, and a cold hand seemed to squeeze my heart. There was a definite sense of eeriness invading the area. I took a shaky breath, pivoted on my heel to confront the uninvited entity, and almost peed my pants in fright.

The *thing* was huge and ugly, and it stood between me and the door. My gaze narrowed in on the green ooze dripping from its gaping mouth, and the red glowing eyes glittering with evil purpose. Its scaly skin appeared grayish-green, and the image of an alligator stalking its prey under the still waters of the Okefenokee Swamp flashed through my mind.

"I have anticipated our meeting since I arrived." The surprisingly lyrical voice broke the silence. Who would have thought a demon's voice could be that beautiful? But then I remembered Lucifer and his charms.

A demon. Well, why not? I'd been consorting with ghosts and heavenly beings. Why not a female demon from the pit of Hell? Geez. My life sucketh greatly.

"I can't say I share the sentiment," I responded in a shaky voice. My knees continued to tremble, and nausea gurgled in my gut. The demon's foul breath brushed over me, and I shivered with dread. "What do you want here?"

"Only to help. I have a proposition that might interest you, my dear."

"I don't need your help."

"Ah, but you do." Leathery wings unfurled, flapped an ugly sound, and then tucked back against its rounded belly. "I've only been waiting for the right time to offer my services. I believe the time has arrived."

In spite of my fear, I was intrigued enough to ask, "Why now?"

The demon only smirked. "The List."

"You know about that?" Surprise heightened my voice, and I thought of Scarlett and Heaven's big kick-ass angels. If I sent out a universal SOS, would they swoop in and rescue me from the facial room beast? Man, this was way out of my scope of understanding, and I needed immediate help from the "Celestial Top Ten"—the best known winged celebrities in the Universe.

Red eyes gleamed with understanding. "I can stop the carnage by placing your mother in my protective custody," the lyrical voice taunted.

My hackles rose in self-defense. Holy crap! I couldn't let this creature anywhere near my sainted mother. Then a flash of inspiration struck, and I made a sign of the cross over my chest. "In Jesus' name, I command you to leave my shop!"

An explosion of sparks rained down from the ceiling in fiery embers, and I jumped back in surprise. When the smoke cleared, the demon only laughed, exhaling puffs of red and yellow, which smelled of sulfur. "Do you really want to engage in a fight with me, my dear? I think not. I'm your only hope of stopping Annie Mae's entrance into the afterlife. And stop throwing around names. It's irritating and has no effect."

I bobbed my head in response. Freaked out and scared out of my wits, I didn't have a clue what to do or say next. The only thing which came to mind was to keep a steady stream of silent appeal to the heavenly realm, while the beast huffed and puffed like that wolf from a childhood fairy tale. Watching those red puffs brought to mind another childhood story, and an idea took shape.

"I guess you have a name?" Sweat peppered my upper lip.

"One that is as old and revered among the gods."

I quirked a brow in consternation. "And that would be?" Come on give it up.

The demon fanned itself with its leathery wings. "My name is unimportant."

"Pretty bad, huh?" I retorted with a snort, hoping she would play my game. I needed that name.

The demon did not deny it. "I was present in the Garden of Eden."

My mind did back-flips trying to recall my Sunday school lessons but came up empty, so I took a wild guess. "The snake?"

"The snake comes late in the story." The beast of the facial room laughed. "I am the wind spirit."

Sheesh! I hadn't a clue. "Well, I know you're not Eve."

An evil chuckle washed over me. "Ah, poor Eve. Subservient to Adam. I refused to lie beneath a man, and because of my rebellion I was banished from my garden paradise."

A memory sparked. No, it couldn't be. Pastor Inman mentioned her once in a sermon at Easter. I made the sign of the cross again over my heart for added protection. "Lilith. Adam's first wife. But you're just a myth."

Again that evil chuckle. "A cover-up for Heaven's mistake, but let's not dwell on the distant past. I'm here to help you stop Heaven's carnage. As I've said, I have

16

a proposition for you, my dear."

In an attempt to banish the evil entity, I made the sign of the cross with my fingers, and commanded in a firm, voice, "Lilith, leave and never come back, in Jesus' name."

This time a shower of sparks flew from her long fingertips to scorch my hair and eyebrows. I felt the sting and jumped back against the wall. Damn, I'd really pissed her off that time, and I let loose a couple of F-bombs as I tried to put out my smoking tresses. From the burning sensation on my forehead, and the foul stench of burning hair, I realized I had paid a hefty penalty for my foolishness, and I had no idea how I would explain my singed condition to my sisters and nosey clients.

I held up a hand of appeal. "Okay, no more name calling. I'm listening."

"Good girl," Lilith muttered mockingly, "you can't win against me."

"And if I refuse this proposition?" I couldn't believe I dared to bargain with one of Hell's angels, but so far no help from above had answered my summons, and I was out of ideas. The dice had been thrown, and I was on my own.

Lilith spit sulfur. "Your mother dies."

At her words, I had a horrific vision of the family gathered around Mama's casket, and I was ready to agree to anything to stop this injustice. "Okay. No tricks, and are you capable of speaking the truth?"

"I am."

"Okay, I'm listening."

"Your soul for your mother's life."

Every hair on my body bristled. "No," was my

immediate answer.

Lilith grinned. "Are you sure? I have it on good authority that your father won't recover from his wife's sudden departure. And what about the others? Billie Jo could lose her son, and Deena may call off her wedding and never love again."

Daddy join Mama in the hereafter? Billie Jo is having a boy! Deena never love again? These thoughts brought me up short. My decision could alter the future, and affect the well-being of my family. But still, I balked. Spending eternity in Hell was a no-brainer. But how could I get my family and me out of this entanglement without one of us, or all of us, paying the ultimate price? I was scared shitless but had to take a chance.

"Would you like some time to consider the consequences?" Puffs of red and yellow smoke filled the room as Lilith laughed with glee. "This proposition is at my discretion."

I jumped on that and crossed my fingers for good luck. "Yes, I want more time."

"And so you shall have it."

"How much time do I have?"

"That is at my discretion."

"And how will I know when my time is up?"

Lilith's red eyes burned with renewed fire. "You'll know, my dear. Don't worry, I'll be closer than you think."

Chapter Three
Bye, Bye, Love

My morning confrontation with Lilith had shaken my confidence, and I wasn't on my game with my next client whose once long brown tresses were now considerably shorter and an ugly shade of bright yellow. As I stood gauging her face in the mirror, she shot me a reproving look.

She dug her cell phone out of her handbag. "I'm going to kill you, Jolene Claiborne." Her quiet, serious tone rumbled with dangerous intent. "I'm literally going to kill you." Tears of rage glinted in her eyes.

Several heads turned our way at her strong rebuke and snickered. Three sets of eyes fixed on me. Flushing with frustration at my lack of concentration, I grabbed up her color card lying on the counter. "Calm down, Lynn. I'm going to fix this with a violet toner." Her face said she didn't believe me, but before I could respond, the front door opened, jingling the bells attached. I glanced over to see Bradford stroll in with a woman clinging to his arm, and head straight for my workstation.

My danger meter sent out a shrill alarm. Oh, hell, more bad luck.

The woman was drop-dead gorgeous. And clinging to Bradford's arm.

That was my first thought as they drew close, and

the woman turned her bright smile on me. She was stunning, with a face to die for, long, curling auburn hair midway down her back, and large, round eyes that glistened like amethysts. She could hypnotize with those violet eyes.

My second thought was to drop her to the floor and rip her face off. Again, my danger meter beeped a second alarm to high-tail it out of there. Instead, I plastered on a plastic smile and told my irate client I would be right back with her toner. She shot me daggers and turned back to her phone. As I walked away, I could hear her disparaging remarks about me to the listener on the other end. With my mood darkening with every passing second, I met Bradford and the beautiful stranger at the reception desk. Thankfully Deena and Billie Jo were exiting from the office at the same time and rushed over. Deena read my down-turned face in an instant and stepped in to ease the building tension.

"Sam, how nice of you to stop in before hitting the road," she gushed with a Grand Canyon smile. "And who have you brought with you?" She turned to smile at the woman.

Bradford cast me a questioning glance, and I knew he too had noticed my singed hair and brows. Not the place to explain, so I remained quiet as he made the introductions. "I ran into this lovely lady out in the parking lot. She's new to Whiskey Creek and plans to open a beauty shop across the street. Ladies, this is Lilith Lacewell. Lilith, this is Jolene Claiborne, and her sisters, Deena Sinclair and Billie Jo Hazard."

The sounds of the salon faded into the background as those amethyst eyes stared into mine. Every hair on my body stood on end, my mouth dried up like old stale cotton, and my psychic sensor zapped me with an electrical current that sent my teeth on edge and my limbs to trembling.

Good God Almighty! It was the beast of the facial room—cleverly disguised as a beautiful woman, like the snake in the Garden—waiting and watching for the perfect opportunity to strike. She'd warned me that she would be close by, but I'd never imagined how close. Damn, too close for comfort.

This called for backup of the heavenly kind— Scarlett Cantrell, and her big kick-ass angels with swords of demon-killing light. Of course, convincing her to help wouldn't be easy. No. Not after our heated pow-wow in the dispensary this morning. She'd been dead set against me challenging the Death Angel, and after strictly warning me to stay out of Heaven's business had vamoosed back from whence she'd come. Gaining her trust and wooing her to back to Whiskey Creek would take time and a whole lot of my evaporating energy.

I tuned back into the here and now and witnessed my sisters giving the ole beasty girl a friendly welcome to Whiskey Creek, and they then turned to me as if it were my turn to extend the hand of greeting. Nope. Since I knew what was hiding beneath that reasonable facsimile of a human being, I wasn't going to shake hands with ole sulfur breath. Instead, I bobbed my head and muttered a hasty hello from a safe distance.

Bradford twisted his hat in his hands, a sure sign of impatience. "Now that you've been properly introduced, I'd like to speak with Jolene privately if you ladies will excuse us."

Deena gave me the thumbs up gesture, and Billie Jo just smiled. Motioning to one of my stylists, who stood gawking from her workstation, I instructed Lizzie to apply a violet toner to my client's yellow tresses while I had a word with Detective Bradford. She gave a quick, flickering nod and headed off to the dispensary.

Wallowing in a pit of misery, I led him to Deena's vacant office and closed the door behind us, before following him over to the sofa where he captured my hand and pulled me down beside him.

"I know I planned to leave at first light tomorrow, but I've decided to head out this afternoon," he said, his tone flat, his eyes expressionless. "However, I couldn't leave without saying a proper goodbye." He squeezed my hand.

"Must you leave so soon?" My voice shook. "Give me time, Bradford. So much has happened this morning. Mama is in—"

"It's okay to say no, Jolene," he cut in. "I understand your commitment to your family, and you've started another relationship. Moving away with me was too much to ask, I can see that now. Especially after that fiasco with Vanessa." His smile faltered.

He was referring to his short-lived romance with Vanessa van Allen—erotica romance writer with sticky fingers and a greedy heart. Bradford's former girlfriend stole another writer's work and paid the ultimate price for her deceit. At last word, she was on trial in the celestial court of justice, but that's another long story told elsewhere.

"Let the past rest, Bradford. That's not why I can't leave. I've been trying to tell you that Mama is in trouble."

His hand tightened around mine. "What kind of trouble?" His blue eyes darkened. "I haven't heard anything through my contacts. Did you call the station?"

I said something incredibly stupid. "Mama's on Heaven's hit list." My voice trailed away as his face drew into a tight frown. He dropped my hands and surged to his feet and moved a few feet away from me.

"Dear God, Jolene. I don't know how you manage to get mixed up in these matters." He scrubbed a hand through his dark hair, the movement calling attention to the growing silver highlights. "I don't believe I can take more paranormal activity. I'm done with ghosts and goblins. Jolene, this is crazy—even for you. Heaven's hit list, really! After that crazy business with Vanessa, you promised to get help for your problem." There was a mixture of disbelief and anger in his voice, but for just an instant, I saw a flash of uncertainty in those baby blues.

"This came up kinda sudden," I tried to explain. "It's not like I plan these things. They just happen." I watched him with narrowed eyes. "And don't forget you have seen a ghost or two so don't rush to judge. I thought you'd understand my situation better after your experience with Vanessa's spirit, but apparently, I was wrong. With that kind of attitude, I believe it would be best for you get on your horse and ride out of Dodge. I need a clear head to deal with Heaven's agents of destruction, and you're just mucking up the stall."

"Is that how you truly feel? You want me to leave?"

Before I could speak, there was a quick tap, and the door opened to admit Deena. "I'm sorry to interrupt,

23

Jolene, but you have a visitor." Her brows hiked high over anxious brown eyes. "He's waiting for you in the kitchen."

I surged to my feet. Without being told, I knew my morning visitor could be none other than Dr. Preston Neally. Geesh, my life was becoming more and more complicated each day.

Bradford grabbed up his hat and shoved it on his head. "I was just leaving." He dropped a kiss on my cheek. "Take care of yourself, Jolene."

Seeing the futility of continuing, I offered a weak smile. "Goodbye, Bradford. Safe travels."

And with that, he dashed out the door and out of my life.

****

Mama blew in later that morning like a late summer hurricane. She sailed into the reception area, slapped her purse on the desk, and flashed my sisters and me a huge smile. "Okay, girls, I'm here. What's next?"

Deena took charge. In just the right pleasant tone, she pointed at Holly. "For the next three days, you will be Holly's shadow. She will train you to run the desk in an easy, efficient manner, and show you how to book appointments on the computer. You will answer the phone and restock the retail shelves. And when needed, you will help out the stylists with prepping their clients for a chemical service. You'll also be the shampoo girl."

"That's a mighty tall order for minimum wage." Mama's voice twanged with disapproval. "You should've mentioned this before I agreed to work for you." She turned to Holly. "I don't blame you for leaving, child, I would too if it weren't for my daughters owning the salon and needin' my help."

Crap. Southern Mamas are a real pain in the ass.

Seeing where this was headed, Billie Jo and I excused ourselves and made for the kitchen. Me for a late morning snack before my next client, and Billie Jo for a glass of iced tea before she returned home for a nap.

After taking a seat beside me at the kitchenette table, she grabbed one of the chocolate chip cookies I'd brought from home and took a bite. "Care to share what's got you so quiet other than this business with Mama?"

"Bradford's left for Wyoming."

"You made your choice?"

I shoved a cookie into my mouth and nodded my head. "Preston."

She gripped my arm. "Oh, Jolene, how could you? You're not in love with him. Sam's the guy for you. What's the deal?"

"Preston suits my needs for now." I shrugged my shoulders and grabbed another cookie. "And what's love got to do with anything? I'm not cut out for the drama that comes with proclamations of undying love. And I'm not moving to Wyoming with Mama's life in danger. Simple as that."

"Horseshit." She beamed at me with false humility. "Sorry. It's the pregnancy hormones. I can't seem to control my tongue."

"That's one explanation." I pushed out of the chair and went to the refrigerator and pulled out bottled water. "The other would be you were born with a sharp tongue and a loose lip, just like me, Billie Jo—and we get it from Mama. Now, can't you see why I made the right choice? Bradford made his choice, and I made mine. End of story."

"End of romance." She shot me a pitiful look.

"Exactly. What matters now is keeping Mama safe and alive, and her feet planted firmly on the ground. Any suggestions."

"None other than the ones we have already discussed." She finished the last of her tea. "Well, gotta shove off. Time for my nap." She stifled a yawn and began to rise.

I lifted a hand to stop her. "Hey, before you go I need to shoot something by you."

She resumed her seat and fixed me with an intense stare. "I knew there was more. You always hem-haw around when something's bothering you."

"It's about Lilith Lacewell."

"Seems nice enough. Pretty too. Although I'm not happy about Lilith opening a beauty shop across the street from Dixieland. We don't need the competition."

"In her case, beauty is only skin deep," I said with a frown. "Underneath that pretty exterior lies a she-demon from hell. Alligator skin and bad breath. Right out of the swamp."

Billie Jo's smile vanished. "Jolene, I'm surprised at you. That's not a nice thing to say or even joke about. Lilith is charming, a real Southern lady." She looked hard at me. "Oh, I get it. You're jealous because she came in with Sam. But you don't want him so what does it matter?"

Raised, angry voices sounded from the front of the shop, bringing us to our feet and out the kitchen door. We rounded the corner to see Mama standing face-to-face with a huge woman clothed in a yellow silk caftan. Both were red-faced and puffing like two banty roosters squaring off in a fighting ring.

Great balls of fire! Diane Downey, the grande dame of Whiskey Creek Elite Citizens, president of Women's League and First Baptist Church Ladies Auxiliary, newest elected city council member, and Mama's best friend and sworn enemy. (This kind of love/hate relationship is an accepted practice here in the South. I share a similar bond with my ghost pal, Scarlett Cantrell.)

"Diane, darling, you go too far," Mama snarled, her upper lip curling unbecomingly. "I won't allow you to sabotage my position in the Ladies Auxiliary."

"As president, I can do anything I want." Diane's face throbbed with anger. "We've voted unanimously to proceed with the project. There's nothing you can do."

Mama's fists clenched. "Thief!"

Holly stood nearby wringing her hands, and Deena gasped and fluttered a hand to her cheek. Both stood clear of the two angry women as did everyone else in the salon. Stylists and clientele twittered nearby as speculation ran amok.

Diane fluttered with dismay. "I didn't steal."

I pushed my way between them. "I'm ready for you now, Mrs. Downey. If you follow me to my chair, we'll get started with your appointment." I glared daggers at Mama. "And you can get back to training."

Both women stared at me with disdain, and Diane looked from me to Mama and back to me. "I'm sorry, Jolene, but I believe I'll take my business elsewhere." She held up a business card for me to see. "Lilith Lacewell is opening her shop across the street. I believe

I'll take my patronage to her. As will most of the women at church once I recommend they make a change."

The front door jingled as Diane exited the salon amid a buzz of voices. My blood pressure spiked, and I wanted to strangle Mama and save the Grim Reaper the time and aggravation of a trip to Whiskey Creek. The subject of my displeasure, however, scooted behind the reception desk and busied herself with answering the phone.

Billie Jo turned on her heel and headed for the back door and Deena for her office. With my client off to greener pastures, I took a walk-in to fill my now blank appointment space. After finishing with her, I took a couple of haircuts and waxing appointments to fatten my paycheck. The rest of the morning passed without incident, and I began to relax.

Until Lilith Lacewell waltzed in out of the blue accompanied by Billie Jo.

Caught completely by surprise, I dropped my scissors onto the workstation counter, stunned and frightened for my pregnant sister's safety, and zeroed in on those smiling amethyst eyes sending out spirals of black light that only I could perceive. The sounds of the salon faded into the background as my spiritual equilibrium wavered under the onslaught of Lilith's evil manipulations. Just under the cosmic current I detected a shift to the left in the vibrational frequency of the angels and sucked in a deep, calming breath as pinpricks of electricity goose bumped my skin and fizzed my hair. If this kept up, I'd be sporting a style from the 60s.

A flash of color to my right caught my attention,

and I turned to see Deena rush out of her office to join the others. I tried to move, to intercept her, but a strange force held me to the floor. I'm not sure I sensed it, or how it caught my attention, but on the top shelf, above Mama's head, a heavy speaker moved closer to the edge. Fighting to overcome my totally unnatural paralysis, I let out a silent scream and struggled to move.

Amethyst eyes burned into mine with evil intent. Lilith inched closer to Mama, her eyes never leaving mine, a secretive smile etching her ruby lips.

I watched in frozen horror as the speaker toppled off the shelf as Lilith, with a shout, reacted quickly, barreling into Mama and knocking her to the floor. The speaker lay shattered on the hardwood floor just feet from Mama. Twice now, in three short hours she had come perilously close to being seriously injured, or worse— killed in a freak accident.

Strike Two had come too close for comfort, and it was up to me to save her from the Death Angel.

And that would be easier said than done. Fighting the invisible world was like swatting gnats with a baseball bat.

Chapter Four
Love Will Keep Us Together

I dropped to my knees beside Mama. "Are you all right?" I gave her a light pat on the cheeks, then checked her pulse. Strong and steady. A little fast, but not alarmingly so after the harrowing mishap. "Mama, open your eyes. It's me, Jolene."

By this time, Deena and Billie Jo and the rest of the shop had gathered around Mama's prone form. "Someone call nine-one-one." Deena's voice rose an octave. "Hurry!"

"I'm on it," a client's voice squealed behind me. Panic laced her voice as she spoke with the emergency operator.

Mama's eyelids fluttered, then opened. "What's going on?" She struggled to rise, but I pressed her back down onto the floor.

""Don't move," I ordered in a crisp voice, my mind tumbling over itself as my psychic radar scanned the atmosphere for any further invisible danger. Not perceiving any, I slid my hand under Mama's head to check for blood. None. Good. "You may have a concussion, so lie still until the paramedics arrive."

Murmurs of agreement rose around us. Both my sisters pushed through the crowd and crouched down beside Mama. "Do as Jolene says, Mama." Concern deepened Billie Jo's voice. Her hands quivered as they smoothed Mama's dress down over her knees.

"Should I call Daddy?" Deena cast me a questioning look.

Mama's eyes grew rounder, and breathing fast, she struggled against the hands pinning her to the floor. "Let me up," she protested. "And don't you dare call and worry your daddy. I'm fine."

"You're not," Deena protested in a loud voice. "If it hadn't been for Lilith's quick thinking, you'd be, well, I don't want to think about it."

I didn't either, because I had to consider that Lilith Lacewell staged Mama's near-fatal accident. What's her game? First promising to protect Mama, and then almost wiped her out with a speaker? I studied the crowd but didn't see the she-demon from Hell. My psychic receptors continued to scan the group for the universal messenger of evil. A chill swept over me as I peered into anxious faces surrounding me. She was here. Evil has a particular feel.

Sirens wailed in the distance, and then closer until a blue and white ambulance pulled up out front. A fire truck followed close behind, and then a police cruiser. Seconds later, the bell over the front door jangled, and the first responders rushed in, dispersing the crowd. Two police officers immediately began to usher people out of the way.

My sisters and I climbed to our feet, and together, we stepped back, giving the paramedics room to work. Through the noise, I could hear Mama's robust tone complaining about the fuss being made over her.

The female police officer—her name tag read B. Rivers—stepped away from her partner and made her way over to us.

"What happened here?" Officer Rivers took out a small notepad and pen from her front shirt pocket.

Billie Jo, eyes as wide as saucers, exclaimed, "It was an accident! That heavy speaker tumbled off the shelf, almost hitting my mother." She pointed to the shattered speaker. "Lilith pushed Mama out of the way and saved her life."

Officer Rivers jotted the information down, then skirted around the broken speaker, and finally glanced up. "It fell from that top shelf?" She asked with staid calmness, but her brown eyes were startled.

"Yes, the top shelf," Deena added. "I'm not sure how it happened. I made sure all the speakers were anchored to the wall. The strap must've broken."

"Anything to add?" Officer Rivers directed her question to me. I had plenty to add but knew my comments and speculations about Mama's *accident* would land me promptly in the psych ward, and I was running out of time. Two attempts on her life were two too many. I had to get a handle on the situation and fast. And I needed Scarlett's help to round up that she-demon from Hell.

"I believe my sisters have given all the pertinent information, Officer," I said, my voice as strained as my nerves.

"This appears to be an accident, but before I wrap this up, I would like to speak with Lilith Lacewell if you would point her out," Officer Rivers said, her brown eyes darted over my shoulder at the patrons and staff seated in the reception area.

"She's the pretty redhead talking with your partner."

I spun my head to glance over my shoulder at

Billie Jo's words, and met the icy gaze of the woman herself.

Yep, just as I suspected. Guilty as sin. Those amethyst eyes said as much as they pierced through me. For a second, another thought set my brain a smoking— what if Lilith was, in fact, the Death Angel, and not the she-demon from the Garden of Eden? What if she'd duped me into believing a lie? And what if I were in league with the enemy? Damn, my head was spinning with unanswered questions, and I had to get Scarlett down here fast if I wanted to derail Heaven's plans.

Officer Rivers halted my disturbing thoughts when she moved over to join her partner and Lilith. I followed, feeling impatient and not content to be left out of the loop. I stood just off to the side, my sleuthing periscope up and zeroing in on Lilith's deceptively sweet voice.

"Yes, Officer Rivers. I would be happy to answer any questions you have, but I've just done so with," here she paused to lay a hand on the male officer's arm. Her eyes and mouth were posed to charm, and her voice twanged with an exaggerated Southern accent I knew to be false. "This here handsome officer. But I'm anxious to be of help, so ask away."

Billie Jo, who stood next to me and heard the exchange, nudged me with her elbow. "Isn't she wonderful? A real heroine." She sighed dramatically. "Admit it, Jolene. You were wrong about her."

Like hell I was, and no way would I admit to anything. I'd spend the night in a viper's nest blindfolded with my hands tied behind my back. For the tenth time this morning, my bloodpressure spiked, and I felt the first pings of a migraine coming on.

"Mama's fine now, Billie Jo. Why don't you go home and get some rest?" I suggested in a strong whisper. "The doctor said too much excitement isn't good for the baby." I laid my hand on her belly. "Perhaps I should call Roddy."

Man, oh man. That did the trick. Billie Jo shot me a frustrated look. "Tattle-telling is for kids, Jolene."

"Adults are just kids playing grown-up, sis." I gave a limp shrug. "And I'm only thinking of the baby. However, do what you want. I'm sure you know better than the doctors."

That last statement brought a flush to her cheeks. "Okay, you win. For now." She stalked off towards Deena and Mama, who was now sitting in one of the reception chairs that had been brought over by one of our patron's.

When I turned back around, Officer Rivers had pocketed her notepad and pen. "Well, not much here to investigate. This was purely an accident." She twirled the business card in her hand. "Thank you for your cooperation, Miss Lacewell, and I'll be sure to stop in for that free haircut when your beauty shop opens."

Since Mama had refused a trip to the hospital, the first responders packed up their equipment and left, leaving the shop buzzing with speculation about her accident. From the way jaws were flapping, I knew the telephone lines would be abuzz in about fifteen minutes, if not already on fire—one of the disadvantages of small town living, but it beats heavy traffic and smog.

Billie Jo had taken my advice and gone home. After light applause from the occupants of *my* beauty salon, Lilith—after receiving a grateful hug from Deena and Mama—waltzed out the front door clothed in the illusion of innocence and humility. Only I could see beneath the beautiful mirage to the monstrous fire-breathing creature waiting to strike at the next opportune moment.

A demon had invaded Whiskey Creek, and I was the only one to recognize that her presence was an omen of disaster. My family and friends couldn't perceive the danger, but I could, and that was all that mattered.

A spark of hope flared, and a plan began to take shape.

****

"Jolene, honey, I asked you here to discuss your mama."

I lifted my gaze from the family of ducks gathered at the water's edge for the bits of bread I tossed at them, to fasten my eyes on Daddy's slumped shoulders. "I figured as much." I looped my arm in his and pressed close to him. "I'm sorry for this morning. I should've been gentler with y'all, but I lost my head. You know I'm not good in a crisis. I tend to fly off the handle and get myself in deeper water."

We were standing on the dirt path that wound around Joggers Pond in the midafternoon. The crisp fall air felt refreshing after the warm, stuffiness of a packed salon. In the distance, the Methodist church steeple rose above the towering trees, their leaves flaming red and gold against the cloudless blue sky.

He patted my arm. "But you always come through in a pinch, honey. That's why I wanted to talk privately with you. I need a better sense of what's going on. Especially after those two fluke accidents involving

Annie Mae."

"Fluke ain't exactly the word I would use, Daddy. They were carried out by Heaven's assassin."

At my pronouncement, Daddy frowned, shaking his head. "This is the hardest part for me to accept, Jolene. Glory be, God doesn't assassinate people!"

"Oh, yes, he does," I argued, my voice rising with every word. "The Good Book confirms it in Job where it says a man's days are numbered, and he can't live longer than the time set. What a bum deal. When your number pops up in the number generator wheel, Heaven sends out the Grim Reaper to cut you down whether you like it or not! In my book, that's assassination."

For a moment, neither of us spoke but allowed the sights and sounds of Joggers Pond to wash over us. I continued to toss bread upon the water while sending another silent universal SOS heavenward, hoping Scarlett might be in the near vicinity and answer my summons. Although to the casual observer I might appear calm, the fact is I was wound tighter than the skunkvine in my front yard.

Since my ghostly sidekick was giving me the silent treatment, I gave Daddy a quick rundown of Mama's situation with *the list*. I left out my interaction with the she-demon, Lilith Lacewell, and my suspicion she had been dispatched to put an end to Mama's earthly life.

Daddy scrubbed a hand over his forehead. "We have to figure this out, Jolene. I can't imagine my life without Annie Mae." He turned to look at me. Tears burned in his eyes. "She's the reason I get out of bed every morning."

I turned away before he could see the fear his words provoked. Up until now, I had been running on nervous energy and outrage, but in this peaceful place with Daddy, intense fear took hold of me. What if I failed to save Mama? And if I did fail, how would her death affect the rest of the family? Mama was the glue that held us together. Losing her would alter our lives forever. Nothing would ever be the same again.

God, I hated change.

And everything was changing around me.

Suddenly a stray thundercloud rolled in, blocking the sunlight and mirroring my mood. A crack of thunder had the family of ducks fleeing as the songbirds ceased their singing, and several nearby mothers with strollers turned and scurried away in the rising wind. My psychic radar kicked on, and I swept the surrounding area for the undead. Across the lake, perched in the branches of the towering trees surrounding the Methodist church, I discerned several large, black lurking shapes. Not birds. Too big. Buzzards? If so, they were the biggest damn buzzards in the state.

A creepy feeling skittered down my back as I continued to survey the atmosphere. A restless, strong and growing evil—designed and purposeful—seemed to be building in the heart of the city. I watched as several more black shapes joined the others in the trees overlooking the lake. Another boom of thunder sounded from the lone cloud.

What the hell?

Daddy tapped me on the arm. "Jolene, I believe we'd better continue this discussion in the car. There's a storm brewing."

I cast an eye heavenward and caught a flash of silver. Not lightning at all. Great balls of fire—Scarlett on her heavenly Harley! From the angle of her descent, she was landing in Peaceful Valley Cemetery. For some unknown reason she had taken to visiting her gravesite once a month, and I was tickled pink at the prospect of going there. If I hurried, I could manage a private chat with her before she disappeared back into the wide blue yonder.

"I need to scoot, Daddy," I said, quickly pulling myself together, my mind already formulating a plea for Scarlett's help with my plan. "Just remember to keep a sharp eye on Mama at all times, and call me if there's a problem. Deena's on guard duty at the moment, and when I get back to the salon, I won't let her out of my sight. Trust me that everything will be okay." I smiled to lighten the mood.

He responded with a half-smile. "I think I'll mosey over to the salon before heading home. I know Roddy's crew has gone over the salon for additional hazards, but I want to check out the reception area for myself."

I trailed him back to his truck and leaned in for a hug and a quick *I love you*. "Tell Deena I'll be back in time for my four o'clock appointment. I have to run an errand."

Daddy didn't comment, just turned, nodded his head, and reached for the ignition. Not waiting, I sprinted to my car and made haste to the cemetery. As suspected, I spotted Scarlett sitting on her marble headstone, humming a musical tune. Her eyes turned downright frosty when I plowed to a stop before her grave.

"Go away, Claiborne," she growled. "You're disturbing my downtime."

"I only need a minute."

"I don't have a minute."

"You have eternity," I reasoned, then added in a feeble voice meant to foster her sympathy. "Please. I need your help. All I ask is one minute."

"Excuse me." She disappeared beneath the grass covering her grave for several seconds, then reappeared. "Still dry, and I'm aging quite nicely, I'm pleased to say."

I shivered at the implication. "So this is why you visit every month? To check for leaks in your coffin?"

"If I don't, who will?" She waved an impatient hand. "And now that that's done, I'll be movin' on to my next assignment. I think I'm headed to the Austrian Alps to bring in a Norwegian stripper. Young and male, of course."

I left that alone. No need to check for brains in an empty noggin. Instead, I made a gesture of defeat. "I guess Mama's doomed to ride the old, black train. Promise me, Scarlett, you'll keep an eye on her when she joins you on the Other Side."

A string of colorful curses lit up the darkening sky, but her fading substance began taking on a more solid form. "Claiborne, you really burn my ass. I can't interfere with fate. Neither can you. So give it up and accept that your momma is fixin' to join the Hallelujah Choir. Bein' dead ain't so bad."

I wrung my hands. "Just check for updates, Scarlett. See if anyone knows how she's gonna be taken out. That's all I ask. Please," I added for extra measure.

She flashed a brilliant red. "Oh no. I'm not going near Hit Squad headquarters. If I'm caught, that's a sure-fire way of me chopping off my own head."

"You get caught?" I shook my head at her in

feigned innocence. "You're too smart for that." I drove home my point. "Why I bet you're the smartest dead person I know. This would be a snap for a PI like you." I snapped my fingers for emphasis.

Scarlett's immense Southern pride took the bait. "Yes," she cooed. "I'm the best at what I do. And, I suppose I could slip in and out of there without anyone the wiser."

"So you'll do it?"

"I'll consider it after I thoroughly scope out the risks."

"There's one more itsy bitsy teenie weenie little thing—"

"You have some nerve, Claiborne." And with a flash of brilliant light, she was gone.

Chapter Five
Stand By Me

Scarlett woke me with dawn's early light peeking through the windows. One minute I was resting peacefully in the placid morning quiet, and then I was wide awake with fireworks lighting up my bedroom like the Fourth of July. I fell out of bed at the first blast and landed on the floor with a definite *thunk*. Apparently, my cat, Tango, had sensed the coming apocalypse and had bugged out for his hideout. Through a curtain of tangled hair, I stared up at Scarlett's wavering spirit hovering over the bed.

"I came as soon as I could get away, Jolene." Her transparency began taking on a more solid form, and I could see she had exchanged her biker threads for a short, white toga costume—complete with gold belt, sandals, bracelets, and a necklace. A golden leaf crown encircled her lavishly styled bronze hair, much like the pictures I'd seen of the Roman Goddess, Venus.

I cocked a brow but made no comment about her weird apparel. "Give me a minute, Scarlett." I pulled myself up from the floor, using the bed, and stumbled into the bathroom to splash water on my face and answer nature's call. I emerged to see her posed dramatically over the unmade bed with a bunch of ripe, purple grapes in one hand from which she was plucking and then popping between her red-coated lips.

Since her antics had ceased to amaze me, I slipped on my robe and made my way to the kitchen to turn on the coffee pot and wait for her to join me.

My wait wasn't long. When I turned around from taking a package of premade waffles from the freezer, she was transposed over the table playing with a small golden harp. That stopped me in my tracks.

"Nice harp," I commented, setting the box of waffles on the counter next to the toaster. "I didn't know you were musically inclined."

"I'm not." Her face crinkled in thought. "I picked it up as a means of stress relief. And I'm really stressed out at the moment."

I pulled out butter and syrup from the refrigerator. "Oh yeah? What's got you stirred up?"

A few notes twinkled from the harp. "You, what else? FYI, you're my problem child."

The look on her face made me want to laugh. "Mama says the same thing, Scarlett. I'm sorry to be the cause of so much stress this morning. Care to tell me why?" I placed cream and sugar on the table alongside the butter and syrup.

"I almost lost my wings last night," was the answer.

"You don't have wings."

"And you're the reason why I don't."

"I pretty sure I'm not responsible." I plopped down at the table while I waited for the coffee to finish dripping. "I believe I'm going to need more in the way of an explanation. However, I prefer you sit at the table like a live person."

She materialized into the chair across from me. "I managed to obtain the information you requested,

Jolene. However, I didn't come out unscathed. And neither did you. I received my last warning from the Boss, and you've been placed on the list of known habitual violators. Not good, Claiborne. Not good at all. You're at risk of losing your eternal status in the Golden City."

I waved an impatient hand. "Can't worry about that now. Just give me the info on Mama."

"She's scheduled to arrive at the Pearly Gates on the seventeenth."

"On Deena's wedding day?" I smacked my hand on the table. "Mama's being assassinated at Deena's wedding? Good God Almighty! This can't be happening." I jumped up from my chair and began pacing across the polished hardwood floor.

"I never said that, Claiborne."

"You said the seventeenth." I fought a surge of anger. "Deena's wedding day."

"But I don't have a time or place or method of extraction."

I stopped pacing to glare at her. "Mama's not a bad tooth, Scarlett."

"Either you calm down, or I'm outta here. I shouldn't be here anyway."

"Wait, don't go. I need the company." I poured steaming coffee into a mug, wishing its heat could chase away the chill invading my bones and turned around to see her perched on the stovetop.

"I'll stay only if you promise to talk about something other than your mother's plight," she twittered. "And don't even think about asking for more help. I'm in enough trouble as it is." A sly smile crossed her foxy face. "Let's talk about you for a change. Tell me how your delicious detective and doable doctor are getting along. Last I heard they were hot on your trail, and you had a choice to make."

The hot coffee tasted terrific, and I took a few more sips before answering. "The delectable detective made it for me. He left for Wyoming yesterday."

"So it's the doable doctor wearing your saddle?" She gave me a puzzled frown. "I'm surprised you settled for second best, Jolene. You're not doctor's wife material at all. Too tame for your taste."

I agreed. "Don't plan on marrying the man. Just dusting off the sheets."

Her smile twisted. "I miss that part of physical life the most. Get it while you can, Claiborne. That's my motto. The best things in life are free and best enjoyed on your back." Here she lifted a haughty brow. "Any regrets?"

"Lots."

I suppose my face was grim because her voice softened when she spoke, "I hate to cut this short, Jolene, but I really should get back to Heaven. I'm on probation, and it wouldn't do for Saint Peter to find out I'm here."

I blinked back tears and set my mug on the table. "One question before you go. What can you tell me about Lilith, the wind spirit?"

She flashed a sickly neon green before settling into a ghostly shade of white. "Why are you asking?"

The fear in her eyes had my insides quivering. "She's here in Whiskey Creek."

"Good Lord, please tell me you're not tangled up with that ancient spirit."

"You're afraid of her?"

"The Devil's Mistress? You betcha I am. She's trouble, Claiborne. Has been since the beginning. She rebelled against the Powers That Be and caused a huge stink. What's she doing here, and how did you hear about her?"

"She invaded the facial room. Remember? It was you who first warned me."

"What does she want?"

I pushed up from the table for a second cup of coffee. "You should know. She's the Grim Reaper."

"Wrong again." She floated over to the counter. "This is bad, Jolene. Real bad. I need to report this to my boss right away. They'll need to dispatch the heavy artillery ASAP. What else do you know about the Queen of Hell?"

"She's disguised as a pretty redhead." I popped in a couple of frozen waffles into the toaster. "She calls herself, Lilith Lacewell. She plans to open a beauty shop across the street from Dixieland Salon. Oh, and she wants my soul in exchange for Mama's life."

"I assume you accepted."

Scarlett's droll words weren't amusing, but I smiled anyway. "I asked for more time to consider the proposition. However, I believe my time is just about up. I would appreciate some help if you'd dispatch a couple of big kick-ass angels as my bodyguards."

"I warned you about the Dark Powers, Jolene. They're bad. Really bad, and you're just the kind of person they covet. Your continued defiance has captured their interest, and it may be too late. The Boss will know. See ya."

With a flash she was gone, leaving me alone with my troubling thoughts but not despondent. Scarlett had given me a definite date of Mama's departure, and I had eight days to figure out how to keep Mama out of Heaven's clutches.

Eight days. Not a lot of time to stop destiny's hand.

****

Saturdays are killers in my line of business, especially when every wasted second can make or break your bottom line for the week. And to my way of thinking, this early morning mission to pick up donuts for the staff meeting was costing me precious minutes which translated into dollar signs.

For the umpteenth time, I glanced down at my watch and heaved a dramatic sigh, my foot tapping out my impatience, earning me several disapproving looks from the other customers standing in line at the new grocery store.

Finally, after several more dramatic sighs, and stern glances from the waiting seniors, it was my turn at the counter. Hastily, I placed my order and tried to look tolerant as the young woman took her bloody time putting two dozen chocolate covered donuts in a bakery box and tying one of those itty bitty strings around it like they used to do when folks moved at a slower pace. I was just about to hurry her along with a few choice words when a slight pressure on my arm had me staring down at a blue-eyed, freckle-faced kid with curls the color of spring corn.

"Ma'am, could you please help me find my momma?" she asked in a surprisingly loud voice for one so young. Every head turned in our direction. Several eyebrows lifted expectantly for my answer.

Holy crap. Another delay. My first inclination was to outright refuse the youngster's request. However, I checked my response. Manners may be slipping a bit in today's society, but make no mistake about it, they still matter here in Dixie. If I failed to help the little tyke find her lost mother, the grapevine would explode with my atrocious behavior in a matter of hours. And that just wouldn't do with the competition opening a salon across the street from Dixieland. The *Golden Rule* reigns supreme, and the old guard kept tabs on those who failed to practice it to *their* satisfaction.

Such are the perplexity of Southern manners.

With a tip of my head, I acknowledged the old dragons frowning at me, and in my sweetest voice, assured the little girl that I would assist her in locating her parent as soon as I received, and paid for my order.

Mrs. Shacklefort, the haughtiest dragon of all, seemed pleased with my answer. Yippee!

I collected the donuts, and the little girl's hand, and went in search of the lost mother. After several minutes of combing the isles, we collided with the frantic woman over in the produce section. From the lecture little Abby received, I assumed she was a habitual offender and was in for a sound spanking when she got home. I accepted the grateful parent's praises and made my escape.

Then, curse the fates, I ran into Diane Downey on Isle 9.

Choking back a few choice cuss words at my incredibly bad luck, I skidded to a stop and faced the old dragon with a plastic smile. "Good morning, Mrs. Downey."

"Good morning, Jolene." Her eyebrows lifted with what I would call a *bitchy* disdain, and she spoke in a slow Southern drawl, "I heard what happened to Annie

Mae yesterday morning at the salon. The Good Book says we reap what we sow, and thankfully, the good Lord has seen fit to hand out a just punishment for her mean treatment of me."

Seeing how I knew Diane hadn't forgiven Mama for launching out on her own and publishing a cookbook, and selling well I might add, I clamped down on my immediate response of her hypocrisy. You see, Diane Downey didn't practice what she preached. Ellie Malone, a former nail tech, had once accused her of being one of them go*od Christian bitches* who looked down on the rest of us poor, lost sinners. In Diane's estimation, the golden rule of reciprocity didn't apply to her. She could stick it to you, but you couldn't stick it back.

"I see you have nothing to say about it," she continued in her squeaky voice. Her lip curled in a snarl, and I stepped back a step to put a little much-needed distance between us. "I'm petitioning the Church Ladies Auxiliary to investigate Annie Mae's atrocious behavior, past and present, and have her removed from the organization. I find myself questioning her Christian ethics."

Okay, the bitch was crossing the line, and I clutched the donut box closer to my chest so I wouldn't give into temptation and cream her with an assortment of gooey chocolate, sprinkled-covered donuts. Just as I opened my mouth to give the old dragon a piece of my mind, my psychic radar zapped me with an urgent jolt of electricity.

Diane let out a screech of jubilant exaltation, "Oh, look, it's Lilith Lacewell!" She threw her hands up in the air. "Isn't she an angel? A beautiful angel from

Heaven?"

My grip tightened on the box, and I looked over my shoulder at the woman innocently pushing a grocery cart toward us. My heated gaze fastened on the redhead—me being the only one who could see the alligator scales beneath her bewitching disguise. Scarlett had referred to her as the Queen of Hell. The name fit. With hair of fire, I could almost smell the stink of sulfur when the woman drew to a stop beside us.

Mrs. Downey was beside herself with enthusiasm for Whiskey Creek's newest citizen. Her face beamed a sunny welcome. "Good morning, Miss Lacewell. As the newest member of the city council, let me be the first to welcome you to Whiskey Creek. We're so looking forward to the opening of your beauty shop, *Shear Indulgence*."

"Salon," Lilith corrected in a soft, cultured voice. "I prefer beauty salon. Beauty shop sounds so, um, Southern, don't you agree, Jolene?"

I snickered at Diane's temporary loss of words until those smiling amethyst eyes settled on me. Goosebumps erupted all over my body, and I caught a whiff of her foul breath. Sheesh. The woman needed a breath mint.

Not in the mood for a public confrontation, I lifted the box of donuts. "I really need to scoot if you ladies don't mind. I have an employee meeting in ten." For Diane's benefit, I gave a quick nod to Lilith. "Thanks again for your part in saving Mama from what could've been a horrible fatal accident, Miss Lacewell. My family and I appreciate your quick thinking."

"My pleasure." The amethyst eyes blazed red as

they burned into mine. "I'm always glad to help a soul in trouble." Her foul breath washed over me with her next words. "Take care of your mother, Jolene. Life is short and unpredictable, and one never knows when your time has run out."

Her gaze burned with renewed fire, but I could read between the lines. My time was up. Lilith expected an answer—now. My soul for Mama's life? I knew my answer, yet still, I hesitated to say it out loud. Eternity is forever, and Hell wasn't on my destination wish list.

Suddenly, as if she could read my mind, and answer, Lilith's red lips parted in a vile smile before turning to Diane as if I didn't exist—which was perfectly fine with me. How much time I had, I couldn't guess, so I bolted for the exit with a hasty prayer and my box of donuts.

Chapter Six
The Great Pretender

The cooler autumn temperatures had the morning shoppers out in full force, and the Saturday traffic in downtown slowed my progress, but the stately courthouse square finally came into view. I was glad to see old Colonial Nathanial Taft still keeping an eye out on the town from his lofty position atop his faithful steed. I also noticed the statue needed cleaning and polishing as it had grown green and dull over the years. The sculpture would provide an excellent subject to discuss with the mayor's wife, who happened to be my first client of the day, and never ceased to stop yapping once her huge butt plopped down on my black leatherette stylist chair.

I whipped around two streets, and pulled onto Love Avenue and around to the rear of the shop, where I spied Preston's shiny new BMW parked beside Deena's green Buick.

"Can the day get any worse?" I muttered as I zipped into my parking space—my mood turning dark like the chocolate glazed donuts resting on the passenger seat. Geez, I needed a break from the male species. Now might be a good time to dump the nice doctor and practice celibacy for a while. If the itch became too much for me to scratch, I could throw my saddle over him for an occasional ride.

In the empty kitchen, I placed the donuts on the table. Coffee was dripping so I assumed Deena and Preston must be in her office. They were. And Mama. She cast me a speculative look the instant I strode through the door. I donned a plastic smile and turned to my audience. "Good morning, everyone," I chirped. "Ready for a busy day?"

Preston rose from his chair to place an arm around my waist. "I wanted more time with you this morning, but I'm shoving off for a short weekend conference in Savannah." He pecked me on the cheek. "I'll check with you later tonight once I check in at The Westin. Sure you can't come with me? I'll be back in town Sunday morning."

I had a vision of moss-hung oaks and shaded squares and delicate French pastries and let out a heavy sigh. Savannah was one of my favorite travel destinations, and I longed to tag along for some much needed R&R in a luxury five-star hotel. I felt my resolve slipping when the delectable vision morphed into Lilith Lacewell sinking her sharp claws into Mama's tender flesh.

That did the trick. No question of my leaving. Besides, I had a packed appointment book and Deena's last minute wedding plans to consider.

"No. I'm sorry, Preston." My frown melted into a smile. "Maybe next time. Deena's wedding is days away, and I need to be here. I am the Maid of Honor."

Preston placed another discreet peck on my cheek, excused himself, and dashed out the door, leaving me staring into Mama's troubled gaze.

"I believe you should've taken him up on the invitation, Jolene," she said in her nicey-nice tone. "We could use a vacation from your schizophrenic claims of my impending death. Humph."

That fried my goat.

I heard the muted sound of the front doorbell jingle. "And I believe you should get out there and do your job, *Mommy dearest*," I replied in a good impression of her nicey-nice tone.

We smiled at one another, but Mama lifted herself up from the chair and made her way out of the office.

Deena and I exchanged looks. She was the first one to break the silence. "I don't believe we're going to make it through this. I never thought I would say this, but having Mama here in the salon is driving me batty. Isn't there another way to keep an eye on her? I'm ready to fire her."

"Yeah, we could tie her to a chair at home and gag her, but Daddy isn't too keen on the idea, so this is the next best thing. Relax, it's not forever, just until after your wedding."

A dreamy look crossed her face. "Mrs. Ryder Matheson. Mrs. Deena Matheson." She wiggled in her chair. "Oh, Jolene, I'm so excited to get married again. You should dive back in. The water's just right."

I made the sign of the cross. "No, thanks, sis. Been there, done that, and it didn't work out. This gal is single till death I do part from this earthly realm. And on that final note, I need to get to work. Mrs. Kent is my first client, glory be and help us all."

"Hey, before you leave I want to remind you of our appointment Monday morning with Cheryl Winters, my wedding planner, and Sonya Jones, the woman I've hired to sing."

"I've never heard of her. She a member of our

church?"

"No. Cheryl recommended her. This will be our first meeting. That's why it's important that you be there."

"Are Mama and Billie Jo coming?"

"What do you think?"

"They'll be there, and so will I. What time?"

"Ten sharp in the church auditorium."

"Call and remind me early Monday morning, okay?"

Deena gave me a thumbs up, and I made my way out of her office and to my station, where I was putting on my apron when the mayor's wife pushed through the front door and yoo-hooed me from the reception area.

"Good morning, Amelia," I said, as she squeezed her considerable bulk into my stylist chair. "How's things down at city hall?" Duty demanded I ask, so I did. Amelia loved the English language and the sound of her voice speaking the lingo. Which suited me because I prefer the client do all the yakking as I concentrated on my job. Au contraire to popular belief, some of us beauticians aren't bobble heads, and I am one who basks in the goldenness of silence. However, this morning I had a subject I wished to discuss at length with her—cleaning up the town's statue.

Before I could broach the subject, she swiveled in the chair, twisting her plump face upward to meet my gaze. "Rumor has it Annie Mae provoked a fight with Diane. Any truth to it, Jolene? Did your momma call Diane a thief? Rumor has it they exchanged blows and Diane came out on top."

Mama popped up just as the last word left Amelia's mouth. They eyed one another like two feral tom cats, and I could see from the other patron's gleeful expressions that they too sensed a catfight in the making, and by God, they'd be sure and not miss any of the excitement. Fed up with the continuing drama unfolding, I grabbed Mama's arm and tried to steer her toward Deena's office. Red-faced, Mama balked and jerked her arm from my grasp. She pinched me hard on the upper arm. "If you don't mind, Jolene, I can take care of Amelia's gossiping tongue in two minutes flat." She pointed a long finger in Amelia's face. "You've been aiming for a fight with me ever since I beat you out of becoming the next president of the Garden Club. You're a damned fool, Amelia Kent, if you tangle with me." She balled her fingers into a tight fist.

The atmosphere crackled and popped with antagonism and jealousy. From the corner of my eye, I caught a glimpse of red hair, and I whipped my head around just as Lilith waltzed across the reception area. Her full lips cracked a satisfied smile as she glided to a stop not far from my station. The smile wasn't reflected in her cold amethyst gaze.

"Oh, Mrs. Kent, I've been looking for you," she purred in an exaggerated Southern drawl, her eyes never leaving my face. "I would be ever so grateful for your help in a private matter. My salon isn't open to the public as of yet so we could talk privately over there. That is if you have the time this morning.

Amelia tore the cape from her neck and heaved her considerable bulk out of my chair like a rocket blast. "Time? Oh, yes, my dear," she twittered gaily. "I have time for you now." She turned a nasty expression on Mama and me. "As God is as my witness, I'll never step foot in this place again." She swung away, moving fast toward the front door.

"Oh dear," Lilith purred deceptively. "I didn't mean to steal your client, Jolene. I'm so terribly sorry." She turned the charm on Mama. "Annie Mae, please tell me I didn't cross any lines." She cupped Mama's hands. "I would never purposely hurt your daughter's business."

Mama bought her horseshit. "Don't you worry yourself none, my dear," she said, patting the she-demon's hand. "I'm ever so grateful to you, Miss Lacewell."

"Call me Lilith," she gushed before Mama could continue. "I feel we're such good friends and all. Don't you?"

"Of course, Lilith," Mama agreed. "You saved my life. I'm indebted to you, and would love it if you would join my family for Sunday dinner? We usually eat around one."

Seeing the grit and determination in Mama's eyes, I bit back the retort I'd been about to make, and silently prayed for wisdom. The more I objected to Lilith, the more she seemed to ingratiate herself with my family. I had to find a better way to expose her true nature. I crossed my arms and settled my eyes on Lilith.

Her gaze lit with satisfaction. "Before I go, I would like a short word with you, Jolene. That is if you don't mind."

Mama looked at me expectantly. I nodded for her benefit and led Lilith to the facial room where I knew we'd have complete privacy. I closed the door behind us and turned to face her with my back against the wall.

"Make it quick. Amelia is waiting for you, remember?" I asked in an even tone, not betraying my revulsion and loathing. I had to play it cool. Outsmart the wily fox and play for additional time.

Lilith plopped down on the loveseat. "I can read your thoughts."

I said nothing, merely lifted a haughty brow. Two can play this game.

"Which will it be, Jolene?" Her foul breath poured over me. "Your soul or your mother's life?"

I waited—scarcely daring to breathe. I had known this moment would arrive, yet had held hope that an answer would come. Finally, I said, "I need more time."

"Time's up." Lilith shed her disguise, arching her back. "Ah, that's better." Leathery wings beat against the walls. "I don't know how you humans stand being encased in that obnoxious skin." A hot, sulfur-scented breeze blew against my flushed cheeks. I recoiled against the door, scared shitless, whispering every childhood prayer I could remember.

"Hell's not so bad." The demon rose to its feet, towering above me, and brushed its coarse wings against my face. "You'll grow used to the heat." She blew out a stream of fire with her laughter. "Or perhaps it's Annie Mae's soul I'll collect."

For a split second, I reconsidered my answer and felt the sting of defeat, then shook my head. No, the decision was made, and I couldn't make the sacrifice. Not even for Mama.

****

Sunday was a disaster. It began in Sunday school when Lilith waltzed through the door looking like a million bucks and took the empty chair next to mine. Bedazzled by her extraordinary good looks, every guy in our *Singles* class encircled her. Which left the other women in the class in a snit. All but for me, of course. I couldn't have cared less if she captured every single chap in Whiskey Creek. After abandoning Mama to the dark side, I felt lower than a junkyard dog. I'd slept none and had awakened in a black mood, punctuated by a splitting headache and burdened conscience.

But Lilith didn't stop there. She cast a spell over the entire congregation, including Pastor Inman. Even Roddy couldn't peel his eyes off her. And even more surprisingly, Billie Jo failed to notice her husband's preoccupation. The only male seemingly unaffected by Lilith's beguiling presence happened to be Ryder, and I believe his immunity sprang from Deena's tight grip on his arm. If his head swiveled in any direction, her nails bit down hard into his tender flesh. Several times I witnessed him squirming beside her on the pew. My sister's smile never withered.

I don't believe a single saint heard one word of the sermon. Every eye remained focused on Lilith and her enchanting smile. What really bugged the hell out of me was the fact that not one glorious saint had enough spiritual insight to see the nasty scaly beast beneath the flawless skin. Not one.

The whole scene made me sick. After the service, Lilith was besieged by parishioners. Which suited her fine, by the wide, catlike smile plastered across her beaming face. When my parents joined me outside on the lawn, I tried to coax Mama into rescinding her invitation to the beast of the facial room, but nothing doing. Lilith was coming to the farm for our Sunday after preachin' meal she said in a strong *don't mess with me today* kinda voice. And I'd better turn my frown upside down, she added with a haughty lift of her brow.

Just as I started to express my displeasure of her unwanted advice, Daddy shot me a narrowed look of concern. He shook his head and made a motion of zipping his lips. I took the hint and backed off. But I wasn't deterred. My mind shifted into high gear, and I came up with another plan. A plan that involved a certain Southern ghost with the charm of a washed-up beauty queen and the bite of a killer bee. I glanced around at the lingering crowd. I could hardly contact the netherworld here on church grounds with so many eyeballs on the prowl. No, I needed to head for the house.

"I'll meet y'all out at the farm after I change," I said in a rush and spun on my heels before Mama could stop me. Confidence renewed, I dashed to my car and fired up the engine and sped toward Pinecone Lane.

Tango met me at the kitchen door and immediately let out an angry yowl as he circled his empty feed bowl. Once I filled it, he shut up, and I shot down the hall for my bedroom. Time was limited, so I shed my dress and hose and slipped into jeans and a comfortable flannel shirt. Barefooted, I resumed the lotus position on the carpeted floor and cleared my mind of all traffic as Madame Mia had taught me.

Hey, wait a minute. Of course, Madame Mia! Hell's bells, why hadn't I thought of her sooner? The beautiful psychic medium would know how to send Lilith back to Hell, and thus stop Mama's premature departure to the afterlife. Encouraged, I sprang to my feet and dashed over to the phone on the nightstand and dialed her number.

The line rang three times, and then her deep, husky voice came over the line. "Good afternoon, Jolene. The heavens are abuzz, don't you think?"

I'd learned long ago to go with the flow when it came to the beautiful psychic. Madame Mia lived on another planet and made recurrent trips to Earth with her accumulated frequent flier miles. Besides, one didn't question Madame Mia's sanity or methods. Not if you wanted her help. And I did.

"I'm so glad you're home, Madame." I twisted the phone cord around my pinkie. "I need your help."

"Yes, I know, my dear," her sensual voice echoed back. "I've been expecting your call and adjusted my schedule to accommodate you around three this afternoon."

I agreed with the time and disconnected the call. My watch read twelve-thirty. Mama would be expecting me at the farm shortly. With not much time to spare, I sent out a silent universal SOS heavenward, hoping Scarlett might be bored enough to answer my summons.

She was and popped in with a psychedelic flash. Not expecting her, I stumbled back and let out a screech of indignation as my butt hit the floor.

"Damn it, Scarlett, can't you shelve the light show?" I frowned at her outstretched fingers.

She arched a perfect brow. "Jolene, my dear girl, would you prefer my absence?" Her eyes glowed with wicked glee.

I scrambled to my feet. "Ah, no, I wouldn't. Please accept my apology. I'm super-duper glad you dropped in. I have a job for you."

"Apology accepted." A glint of suspicion seeped into her eyes. "I hope it has nothing to do with your mother because...well, I've been warned by my superiors to avoid the conflict."

The absence of her usual Southern dialect had me doing a double-take. My gaze roamed over her priggish attire and settled on the black-rimmed glasses perched low on her pert nose. All she needed to complete the intellectual guise was a steno pad and pen.

"What's with the getup?" I pointed to the knee length skirt and pumps. "You look like Mrs. Doubtfire with your blouse buttoned up to your chin. I liked the biker mien better."

"I did too, but someone lodged a complaint." Her full lips pouted. "The Boss wasn't open to discussion and suggested a wardrobe change. I remembered old lady Clark from fifth grade English, and," she waved a hand, "presto. The new me."

"It's kind of creepy on you," I pointed out. "Not at all like the real Scarlett Cantrell I know and love."

"Cut the crap, Claiborne, and tell me about the job."

"It'll take some time to explain, and I'm running late, and you know how Mama can be when one is late for Sunday dinner." I slipped on my boots and grabbed my shoulder bag. "I get to do the dishes, and that's not a pleasant way to spend an afternoon. Can you ride out to the farm with me? There's someone I'd like you to meet."

Scarlett nudged her glasses higher and resumed her haughty demeanor. "I believe that can be arranged. But mind you, I don't have all day, and this better be good."

I pictured Lilith and Scarlett together in the same room and couldn't help but smile. "Oh, it's good all right. Take my word. This is one meeting you'll never forget."

Chapter Seven
Smoke Gets In Your Eyes

Fireworks began the instant I crossed the threshold into Mama's kitchen. Like a cat stalking a baby bird, Lilith picked up on my invisible companion and froze, her amethyst gaze zeroed in on the speck of light riding on my shoulder. Electricity zapped me as Scarlett's nails bit into my flesh.

"You could've mentioned the Devil's mistress was coming to dinner." I heard her hotly whispered words through a filter of dense spiritual smoke. "If I come out of this alive, I'm going to kill you myself. The Queen of Hell is trouble, and now she knows I'm here. This isn't good, Claiborne." She continued to breathe down my neck with her words, "No, this isn't good at all. Shit, I'm toast!" I winced as her nails scraped my shoulder blade.

Looking back, I should've realized my mistake. One never brings a lighted match to a bonfire unless you intend to light the fire. Well, in my blonde stupidity, that's exactly what I'd done—brought an inexperienced spirit into direct contact with an ancient demon with a massive chip on her scaly shoulder.

The heat intensified as we three stood locked in silent battle. Lilith's gaze turned a fiery crimson red, and I could think of no way to end the standoff. In the background, I could hear Mama and Daddy chatting away, and I could even smell the fried chicken sizzling on the stove over the stench of Lilith's sulfurous breath. Deena buzzed by me, but I couldn't grasp the meaning of her irritated demand for me to move my big behind out of the way so she could use the powder room. From the fog anchoring me to the floor, I even heard the front doorbell ring.

As if on cue, the skillet of boiling grease ignited into flames.

Mama screeched and dropped the tongs into the skillet. A tongue of flame flared and caught her cotton sleeve on fire. I couldn't breathe or move. Through the chaos of scrambling bodies, I watched in frozen horror as Daddy shoved Mama out of the way and slapped a lid over the flaming skillet. Thinking fast, Ryder splashed a pitcher of water over Mama's torso, effectively dousing the fire.

Looking stricken with shock, she stood dripping water onto the kitchen floor.

I snapped out of my paralysis and felt the psychic energy in the room collapse. Without looking around, I knew Scarlett had blown the joint for safer spaces. So much for Heaven's help. I was on my own with the beast of all beasts.

Seeing Mama standing numbly in the center of the kitchen, I zipped to her side. "Dear God, you could've been seriously burned," I exclaimed through tears of relief, my hands examining the red skin beneath the scorched sleeve. Daddy, Billie Jo, Deena, and Ryder huddled around us.

Daddy scrutinized the patch of blistered skin on Mama's arm. "You're going to the emergency room and have that burn tended to."

"But my dinner," Mama protested. "We have a guest. I can't run off because of a simple burn."

Behind Daddy, Billie Jo spoke up. "Lilith will understand, Mama. We can invite her out another time. Besides, dinner is ruined."

"Who was at the door?"

I lifted my gaze to Deena. "What door?"

The front doorbell buzzed again. "That door," she replied.

Roddy detached himself from Billie Jo's side. "I'll get it," he said and disappeared around the corner.

"Excuse me, but Billie Jo is right in saying that I should leave," Lilith said in a soothing, almost hypnotic voice from the table. "This is a private family affair," she said with a disarming smile. "I can take a rain-check and return at a better time when Annie Mae has recovered from her unfortunate accident." Here her lips stopped moving, but I could hear her voice loud and clear as her gaze bore into mine. *Just a little reminder of who you're fucking with, Jolene. You made your choice, now live with it. Stay out of my way, or you'll be sorry. And don't bother me again with puny spirits from the Golden City. They can't stop me. No one can.*

Holy crap. My plan had backfired. If I'd spooked easily, I'd have turned tail and beat it in a hot second. However, my feet remained frozen to the floor, and I knew I had to hang in there a little longer. I felt stymied but not completely defeated. Madame Mia waited in the wings. Hopefully, she could steer me in the right direction when I met with her at three.

I clenched my fists at my sides. For my family's sake, I forced myself to return her smile, and said in an equally saccharine voice, "Thank you for being so considerate, Lilith. We'll give you a call and reschedule when the time is right."

Without a backward glance, she sailed out of the kitchen door. Immediately, the atmosphere cleared, and Scarlett dropped through the ceiling to settle cozily on the overcrowded shelf near Daddy's corner chair.

"Sorry about that," she said with a twisted smile. "But the Devil's Mistress is way above my pay grade. However, the better question would be are you ready to die?" Her brows arched in amused contempt. "I warned you about the consequences of deceit, Claiborne, and you deceived me. Big time." Her blue-green eyes shone with malice.

I paid no mind to her blustering as I'd heard the threat before. Since entering the Pearly Gates, Scarlett had proved to be all bark and no bite. No, I was safe from her retribution for the moment. Satisfied with the status quo, I switched my attention back to Mama and the others.

"I ain't goin' to the ER," she was saying. "I'm fine. Just a slight burn."

Daddy swelled up like a bloated toad. "You're a-goin', Annie Mae. My word is law in this house."

The old, familiar stubbornness radiated from Mama's eyes. "Who says, asshole? Last time I checked my name was on the deed."

"A minor oversight, mind you," Daddy puffed. "And one I intend to correct tomorrow morning, but first you're goin' to have that burn looked at."

"Daddy's right," Deena broke in. "It could be serious. Let's have it checked out for peace of mind."

"Nope," was her quick reply.

Billie Jo touched her stomach. "Do it for the baby."

Mama peered at her from under her bushy brows and heaved a heavy sigh of resignation. "Okay. For the baby."

Seeing her beaten expression, I had a sudden inspiration. "Why don't I call Preston and see if he'll swing by on his way in from Savannah?"

With everyone in agreement, I waited until they moved into the den off the kitchen before phoning Preston and giving him a shortened version of the incident. Since he'd just arrived back in town, and wasn't far from the farm, he agreed to come on by.

"He's on his way," I said after joining them in the den. "He'll examine the burn and treat it here if it's not serious. However, there's a chance he'll want to take Mama to the hospital for further treatment. I had to promise him that you'd cooperate, Mama."

Soft footsteps echoed from the foyer, and I looked up to see Roddy and Jimbo White enter the room. Daddy pushed himself up from his recliner and grasp the peanut farmer's hand in a welcoming handshake.

"What brings you out on Sunday, Jimbo?" Daddy ran a hand over his chin, looking weary.

The farmer doffed his hat and gave a silent nod at Mama. "I was wonderin' if you and the Missus had given any thought to my offer to buy the farm," he answered in a deep bass voice. His weathered, sun-beaten narrow face was sharp and confident, and his blue eyes were fixed in a permanent squint from long hours working outdoors. He wore baggy overalls over a shirt of wrinkled cotton and well-worn boots.

The usual getup for a hard-working peanut farmer in South Georgia.

"We're not sellin'," Mama said from her rocking

chair. "Not now, not ever." She winced in pain as she thrust a finger at Jimbo. "The matter is closed."

"Are you lookin' to raise the price?" The farmer's bass voice rose a fraction. "If that's the case, then you're wastin' your time." He took a step closer to Mama's chair. "I gave you my best offer, and you won't get one penny more from me."

"Not to me you didn't," she huffed. "Selling the farm is Harland's idea. The only way I'll leave this house is laid out in a coffin."

"Mama! Don't say such upsetting things," Deena's voice rose in dismay.

"Let me handle this," Daddy ordered. "Jolene, you and your sisters help your momma to bed. Dr. Neally will be here shortly."

From the thunderous expression on Mama's face I knew the mountain was fixin' to blow her top, so I shot up from the couch and motioned for my sisters to follow suit. It wouldn't do any good for Mama to become more riled, and I meant to keep Mama from further harm. Even from herself.

I'd barely reached her side when, from my peripheral vision, I glimpsed Scarlett waltz through the wall and was now only inches from my face.

"I believe I'll wait for you at Madame Mia's." She peered at me over her wire-framed glasses. "I'm in a playful mood after escaping the evil clutches of the Hell Hound, and I hear the Madame is conducting a séance with a lively group from the senior center." She clapped her hands together. "I love old people. They don't scare easily, and I need the practice for next Halloween."

With so many pairs of eyes glued on me, I could only give her an almost imperceptible shake of my head and watch her vanish back through the wall. I had given her a quick rundown of my earlier conversation with the Madame on our drive out to the farm.

Mama didn't want to go to bed, and I began to feel the exhaustion and hunger creeping up my body and released a tired sigh. "Well then, perhaps I'll go into the kitchen and rustle up some sandwiches for everyone. Deena and Billie Jo can referee this fight."

"There's not goin' to be any fight," Daddy countered, then turned to face Jimbo. "When we approached you about buying the farm, we were unaware of Billie Jo's pregnancy. With the expected arrival of a new grandbaby, our position has changed. I'm sorry, Jimbo, but the farm is no longer for sale. I hope we can continue with our present arrangement."

Jimbo White slapped his battered hat down on his straw-colored waves. "We'll see about that, Mr. Tucker. I'm not sure I want to continue my association with you folks. I've leased your land for years now, and we've gotten along fine until now. I rustled up all my financial resources to buy those fields, and now you're backin' out. I need this land and house to grow my business and family. Can't say for sure what I'm goin' to do, but there will be repercussions, Mr. Tucker. You can bet your life on that. You'll be hearin' from me soon."

With those parting words, the man left, leaving a vacuum of silence in his wake. Ryder, from his position on the couch, frowned, shaking his head. "I'm afraid he's going to try and break his leasing contract with you. If he succeeds, that could mean a significant financial loss, Mr. Tucker. It may take some time to find another farmer willing to lease your fields. Do you have enough put away in case he follows through with his threat?"

Daddy wrung his hands. "The answer to your question is no, Ryder. Our rainy day fund is experiencing a drought. We depend on those fields being leased. That's the bulk of our income, and it takes just about every penny to keep this place in the black."

"Don't you worry none, Harland," Mama piped up. "You've got to have faith that God will carry us through."

"Faith won't pay the bills, Annie Mae." Daddy's voice sounded tired. He flashed me a grim smile, and my heart sank because I had no answers to give him.

Outside I heard a car pull up, signaling Preston's arrival. Glad to get away from the strained atmosphere, I bolted for the back kitchen door. Needing a breath of fresh air, I swung out of the house and ran over to Preston's white Lexus SUV just as he was climbing out the driver's side. Without thought, I clasped him to me in a sudden bear hug, needing his dependable arms around me. Suddenly, Bradford's parting words echoed in my mind bringing sudden tears.

God, I needed a hero and Preston had answered the call.

Tilting my head back, I peered into his compassionate face and felt my twinkie pie stir with interest for the first time in days. "Are you free later tonight?" I inquired with a husky voice.

He grinned. "If everything goes well with your mother, and I have no emergencies, I can swing by around ten. What do you have in mind?"

For an answer, I placed his hand over my left breast. "A complete checkup, doctor. Bring your stethoscope. My heart is racing like a new convertible."

Our lips met. My twinkie pie zinged, and all thoughts of ghosts, demons, and Pearly Gates faded away in anticipation of a much-needed workout with a man of great stamina and a slow hand. Tonight, I would engage in some good, old-fashioned sex with a younger man who sailed under the false hope that someday he would put a ring on my finger. For now, I'd allow him some leeway because I needed the stress relief, but sooner or later I'd have to cut him loose so he could find a more willing matrimonial partner.

Reluctantly we broke apart, and Preston grabbed his medical bag out of the back seat. "Your mother seems to be living under a dark cloud these days, Jolene," he remarked as he slammed the door shut. "That or she's the luckiest woman on the planet."

I chewed on that a minute as we made our way to the back kitchen door. I paused with my hand on the doorknob. "It's a little of both, Preston. She's been lucky at dodging the black cloud, but I'm afraid one of these days her luck is going to run out."

"I was only kidding, Jolene."

"Yeah, well, I'm not." I flashed a grim smile, then pushed open the door and led Preston into the den where Mama and the others waited. He examined the wound, and thankfully, the burn wasn't severe, but for precaution purposes, Preston administered first aid and bandaged the wound.

"Call my office in the morning for a follow-up appointment, Mrs. Tucker," he advised as he gathered his supplies and returned them to his medical bag. "I can call in a prescription for pain medication if you think you'll need it, but over the counter pain meds should be sufficient at this time."

Mama downed two OTC pain pills, and pleased with all the attention she was receiving, declared she was in the mood for a pizza. Everyone agreed, and while Deena went to call for delivery, Daddy and I walked Preston out to his car. After thanking Preston for the hundredth time, Daddy went back into the house, and Preston left for another appointment. Seeing the time, I jumped in my Mustang and headed for Madame Mia's.

Chapter Eight
This Magic Moment

At precisely three o'clock, Madame Mia met me at the front door of her Fifth Street Victorian mansion. One glance at the frazzled psychic and I knew Scarlet had indeed dropped in to party with the old folks.

"I'm so glad you're here, Jolene," she said, minus the heavy, exotic accent. "An odd occurrence in the séance room has me running late." She swung the door wider and stepped back. "Please come in."

I gave her the once-over. "Would you like to reschedule?" Usually calm and wellput together, the beautiful psychic appeared rumpled and outofsorts standing in the foyer in wrinkled white linen pants and blouse—her raven hair frizzed and windblown. A flush of color stained her flawless cheeks, and I could barely smell her signature scent of lilacs.

My hostess made a face. "Oh, no, just an overactive poltergeist crashed my appointment and upset my clients. Nothing to worry about. I sent the mischievous spirit on its way. However, the reading room is trashed, so if you'll follow me, we'll have tea and crumpets in the sunroom and talk about your special problem." She smoothed down her ebony hair with a trembling hand and closed the door behind me when I stepped into the immaculate foyer with the shining inlaid wood floors and towering twelve-foot coffered ceiling, sporting a huge, ornate crystal chandelier.

Crumpets? I searched my memory for any reference of them. Nope. None. Hadn't a clue what they were and how to eat them. I sincerely hoped whatever they were, they were sweet and crispy like a shortbread cookie. Or a lemon snap.

Madame Mia led the way to the back of the restored Victorian. Following in her wake, I tried not to gawk at the expensive antiques and glorious artwork lining the walls as we passed through spacious rooms. The last time I was here, I didn't see this part of the house. Whatever profession her husband dabbled in, it must be profitable because the mansion was outfitted topnotch. We passed through the kitchen, I couldn't stifle a gasp of admiration when we entered the sunroom.

Now, here was my idea of the perfect winter getaway. The afternoon sun streamed through a three-sided wall of shining glass to spill upon the washed silver oak inlaid wood floors, pale and gleaming. White wicker furniture with teal blue cushions arranged in an intimate seating offered a comfy place to soak up the warm sunshine. Nearby, delicate ferns and flowering plants hung from brass poles placed strategically about the room to catch the warming rays of the sun. Overhead, a fan moved sluggishly, barely stirring the balmy air. In the corner, used for heating purposes, stood an old-timey wood stove and a beat-up tin firewood bucket.

The room was utterly charming, and I coveted every square inch unashamedly. From a splash of water in the nearby kitchen, I measured Madame Mia's progress on tea preparation and wandered over to the wall of glass to admire the outside enclosed garden. Here fall had begun its annual striptease dance, and leaves of red and orange floated seductively to the ground in the gentle afternoon breeze.

Several minutes passed before a low-pitched whistle emitted from the kitchen followed by the rattle of wheels on the wood flooring. I turned as Madame Mia appeared in the doorway between the kitchen and sunroom. During her absence, she had restored her appearance to its usual flawless perfection. One would never guess from her impeccable attire that she'd tangled with my mischievous ghostly sidekick not too long ago. I guess Whiskey Creek's resident psychic was used to otherworldly manipulations. I crossed my fingers that she'd be able to steer me in the right direction with Lilith. Madame Mia was my last hope.

Taking a seat on the sofa, I remained silent while she poured a cup of steaming amber liquid from the glass teapot, and gathered my thoughts on how best to approach the subject of the ancient wind spirit.

With great care, I took the teacup and saucer from my host and added three heaping teaspoons to the pungent brew and a smidgen of cream. I lifted the cup, tested the temperature, and then sipped the tea as I had learned to do while visiting Barbara Herrington in hopes of fishing out answers to her husband's untimely departure in which Daddy had been unjustly accused. However, that interesting story is told elsewhere and definitely worth reading.

Seeing the platter of what looked suspiciously like buttered English muffins, I bypassed them and reached for a lightly toasted sugar cookie. Nibbling on the tasty treat, I waited for Madame Mia to begin the conversation.

Madame Mia's ebony gaze settled on me over the rim of her teacup. "The spirits of Whiskey Creek have been very active this week, Jolene. I wasn't surprised at all to receive your urgent call. The trouble began on Halloween."

Time to get down to *real* business. This magic moment was speeding by, and I had little time left. I gulped down the cookie, set the teacup and saucer on the table, and met her gaze. "I have an unwelcome guest residing in my facial room, and I need your help evicting her."

"Her?"

"A real beast. She claims to be Adam's first wife, Lilith. Know anything about that?"

Her eyes widened in disbelief. "Are you sure it's Lilith? It could be an imp disguising itself. They're extremely active around this time of the year and love to pull vicious pranks. I can't imagine Hell deploying their mightiest artillery to a small town like Whiskey Creek. Most likely you're mistaken."

"I'm pretty sure this is no imp." I grabbed another thin cookie off the dessert tray and shoved it in my mouth.

Madame Mia tapped the side of her face with a manicured finger. "I must consult my crystal ball." She stood. "Come Jolene, tea time is over."

Crystal Ball?

Since when?

I picked my jaw up off of the ground after this stunning revelation. Since I'd never seen a crystal ball during any consultations with the beautiful psychic, I was curious. "How does this crystal ball thing work, Madame? You've never used it before in your readings with me. I need a strategic plan of action, not another lesson."

"That's because I was doing a reading with the Tarots, my dear. This is different."

"How so?"

"To gain mystical insight I must perform the ancient art of scrying—or as you may know it—crystal gazing or crystallomancy. The crystal will allow me to see psychic visions or impressions. I will then seek the wisdom of my guide for the interpretation. All will be well, my dear. You shall see."

Her explanation failed to penetrate my dense ignorance, and I was just as clueless as when I stepped through the front door, but I had no other options to explore, and I was hoping she would extract me from the invisible powers plaguing me like an infestation of mice. There was no one else for me to lean on. Crossing my fingers for good luck, I swallowed the last few drops of tea and pushed myself to my feet. Ready to get this over with, I tagged behind the Madame until we entered the familiar reading/séance room. I paused in the doorway to survey Scarlett's handiwork. Antique chairs were overturned, rugs bunched up and twisted together, candles, bread and fruit littered the floor, and the lacy tablecloth hung from the chandelier. No wonder Madame Mia had appeared frazzled. It must've been one hell of a party Scarlett had with the old folks. I'd be sure and reprimand Scarlett for her outrageous behavior next time she dropped in.

I sucked in a breath. "Wow. Was anyone hurt?"

"Only my pride," the psychic supplied as she

righted the table and chairs. "The seniors were thrilled with the naughty poltergeist, and promised to return for another session." She picked up a blue stone ball lying on the floor and placed it on the table. "They left a hefty tip, so perhaps I shouldn't complain, but I hate losing control of a séance. Not good for business." She moved over to a cabinet and withdrew a black velvet cloth.

I let that pass and pitched in restoring the room back to a semblance of order. The sooner the psychic could focus her attention on Lilith, the sooner I'd have the necessary answers of removing the she-demon from my facial room and Whiskey Creek. And answering a ton of questions crowding my overworked brain cells.

Finally, we took our seats at the velvet-draped table with the crystal ball taking center stage. Mesmerized by its beauty, I could only stare in awe, and a touch of fear, at the shimmering celestial blue sphere, encircled by a hazy white halo. Although I knew it was a trick of the eye, the sphere seemed to pulse with a life of its own on its four-pronged golden pedestal.

Madame Mia must've noted my frozen gaze on the stone ball for she said in her heavy, exotic accent, "The Lapis Lazuli sphere symbolizes royalty and honor, Jolene. Man has sought it above all stones for its link to the gods and their power. Through its use, we find wisdom and truth. It will provide protection from the evil eye, and counteract the wiles of the spirits of darkness and procure the favor of the spirits of light and wisdom."

I gnawed my bottom lip. "Evil eye? Holy crap, I'm going to drape myself in the stuff. If there ever were a person in need of the favor of the spirits of light and wisdom, that would be me. I attract evil like dogs attract fleas."

Ignoring my outburst, she drew the blue sphere from the center of the table until it was just opposite her. "Let us concentrate together on the stone of truth." She inhaled a long breath, then exhaled slowly. "Follow my lead, Jolene and open yourself to the universal harmony. Breathe in, breathe out. Yes, that's it. Just as I taught you. Clear your mind of all thoughts. Be in the present, my dear." She closed her eyes and continued her deep breathing.

Unsure of what to expect with the introduction of the crystal ball, I followed her example but kept one eye cracked open for security purposes. It's never a good idea to completely trust one's physical and mental well-being to a beautiful psychic with dyed hair, a fake accent, and a blue crystal ball. Especially when the Queen of Hell has a target on your back and might pop in without notice.

With one eye on Madame Mia and the other shut tight as instructed, I waited for the next move when suddenly she opened both eyes, grasped the blue sphere in her hands, and gazed intently at the blue ball.

"The undercurrent stirs."

"Can you see Lilith?" I leaned forward, intrigued by this new paranormal device. Not that I'd myself ever indulge in crystal gazing or scrying as Madame Mia had called it.

"No, a woman in a blood-stained wedding gown. She's crying."

I sat up straight. "It must be Deena—she's getting married this Saturday! Scarlett said Mama's departure date was scheduled for the seventeenth. Can you tell me how it happens? How I can stop it?" Ice ran through my veins.

"One can't alter the future, Jolene. Surely, you realize that destiny can't be changed?"

I let out a long exasperated breath. "That may be true, Madame Mia, but I aim to try. Now concentrate and tell me what you see. Is it Mama's blood?" Outside a dog barked in the distance, and a car roared down the street.

She paused, then lifted woeful eyes to peer across the table at me. I tensed.

"No, it's not your mother's blood I see, Jolene. It's yours."

****

I drove home in a stupor. I'd pulled over once by the Quickie Mart, afraid that I might be sick, and bought a soft drink to settle my stomach. Later, when I finally parked my Mustang in the carport and killed the engine, a little shiver ran down my spine. For a moment I just sat there wondering how I'd made it home in one piece with Madame Mia's prediction still ringing in my ears. When I tried to open the driver's door, my arms felt like anchors, and my eyes like the sandy Georgia coastline after a Cat 5 hurricane had blown through.

Inside, I dumped my shoulder bag on the kitchen table and dug the step stool out of the walk-in pantry and butted it against the cabinets beside the refrigerator. With one hand I shooed Tango off the clean counters and opened the top cabinet where I kept the hard stuff. Finding what I was searching for, I pulled the bottle of Tequila from the cupboard and set it down on the counter. From the frig, I found an old lime and sliced it, then downed two shots of Tequila before succumbing to

Tango's yowls for food and filling his bowl with kitty crunch.

Numb with shock and disbelief, I took the bottle of liquor and the lime and settled down at the kitchen table and poured another shot. I downed it and immediately poured another. The fourth shot kicked in, and I felt my world settle into a nice warm, fuzzy cocoon. Kicking off my boots and socks, I stumbled into the den and slipped a jazz CD into the Bose stereo and settled back into the music to forget my troubles. Content with the mesmerizing vocals of the blues King and the liquor streaming through my bloodstream, I felt my eyelids grow heavy.

I awoke to the sound of rapping at the back kitchen door. Startled by the interruption, I popped up from the recliner and staggered dizzily to my feet and almost landed on my ass. Holding onto the recliner until the room stopped spinning, I tasted a backflush of lime and tequila. I gagged but managed to swallow back my last shot. It felt like I'd just fallen asleep minutes before, but the inky blackness of night let me know several hours had passed.

"Wait a minute," I called out as the banging mimicked my throbbing temples. "Hang on, I'm coming."

I switched on the overhead light as I entered the kitchen and hurried to the back door to turn on the outside porch light. Illuminated by the bright light, Preston stood on the bottom step with his stethoscope looped over his neck and a crooked smile plastered on his young, silly face.

"Oh, geez, why can't I go celibate," I groaned through the hangover, remembering our earlier plans to meet up after his hospital rounds, and sent up a silent prayer for a small sinkhole to swallow my amorous admirer and relieve me of the chore of a quick lay—because that's what it would be—a quickie. I was in no mood for sex or even company for that matter. Things were falling apart fast, and I needed to put the pieces together myself. Madame Mia hadn't been much help today but promised to keep her eyes and ears open for any word or sign from the Other Side. As I was leaving her house, she'd cautioned me to stay away from Lilith until she could consult with her friend, who happened to be a demonologist, from Angel Falls, Idaho.

I was tempted to turn out the light and leave him standing on the doorstep in the dark, but I gave into my good nature and opened the door. Preston took two leaping steps, swept me into his arms and squeezed my tushie. His mouth crashed down on mine, and he sucked my tongue deep into his mouth. All thoughts of resistance took a hike in the heat and pleasure of the moment, and I melted against him.

His lips left mine. "You taste like lime and tequila," he whispered into my ear, "and I suspect you're a little drunk. I hate to renege on a promise, but I have to consult with another doctor on a complicated procedure scheduled for tomorrow morning. I can't stay and play with you."

Tango yowled from beneath the table before scrambling for the den. I was just about to protest Preston leaving when Scarlett's unmistakable voice whispered in my other ear, "Ditch the dude, girlfriend. I've got important news from Heaven."

That was all the incentive I needed, so I smacked Preston on the butt and sent him on his way. After locking the door behind him, I shut off the porch light and turned to face Scarlett who was enviously eyeing the lime and tequila bottle.

"That's another earthly enjoyment I really miss." Her sigh echoed through the kitchen. "What I would give for one shot of the good stuff. Tie one on just one last time. Lucky you, girlfriend." Her voice dropped to a whisper.

I massaged my throbbing temples and went over to the window sill and grabbed the bottle of aspirin. "Be thankful you're not in my shoes, Scarlett. I had one too many." From the faucet, I filled a glass with water and downed the pills. "Now tell me the good news from above. I sure could use some right about now. You wouldn't believe what Madame Mia saw in her crystal ball. About me, I mean."

Still focused on the bottle and lime, Scarlett hardly paid me any mind. Taking pity on her, I poured another shot and offered her the glass. "Go ahead and do it so we can get back to my problem. I'm sure it can't do you any harm, you know, since you're dead and all that."

Scarlett shifted her gaze to me, then back down at the shot glass. "I'm tempted, but it's strictly forbidden. If the Boss finds out I've taken a drink…well…well, it won't be good, believe me."

I shrugged. "So don't then." I placed the shot glass on the table and plopped down on one of the chairs. "Okay, Preston's gone, and I'm listening. What's the important news from Heaven? Have they removed Mama's name from the list?"

"No," she answered, her eyes never leaving the shot glass. She fingered the glass. "She's still scheduled to arrive on the seventeenth."

"So nothing's changed?"

"Not with your mother." She picked up the glass and sniffed the liquor. "But the Boss has dispatched his finest team of specialists to scope out Whiskey Creek and find out what's up with Lilith."

"I could fill him in if you'll get him down here."

She removed her glasses. "Impossible. The Boss never leaves his post. He'll know what to do about Lilith. Problem solved." She finally looked up at me. "Do you suppose I could?"

I nodded. "Nothing's stopping you."

"Here's to you." She downed the liquor, sucked the lime slice, and made happy noises. "Damn, that's good. I believe I'll apply for another lifetime. If accepted, I'm coming back as me again."

I let that comment slide. "Is that all you have?" I asked, disappointed with her important news that was really no help at all in the scheme of things.

Scarlett held out the glass for more. "I told you help is here, what more do you want?"

"Don't you think you've had enough?"

"One more for the road." She hiccupped.

I tipped the bottle over the glass, filling it to the brim. "You really shouldn't drink and drive, Scarlett— even a heavenly Harley."

She downed the shot. "I'm not on my Harley. It's in the shop for a new paint job. I caught the ten o'clock shuttle on the Galaxy Express. They dropped me off on the roof. Like Santa."

I almost whipped back a quick "Stop bullshitting me" but decided she might not appreciate me pointing out the lunacy of her statement. Instead, I motioned with the bottle that I'd be happy to pour her another shot.

She took me up on my offer, and I refilled the glass.

"Here's to Deena and the dumbass finally tying the knot." She lifted the glass in a salute, downed it, and then slammed the glass down on the table. Her eyes glazed over. "Oh, I believe I'm forgetting something."

Her words were slightly slurred, but I jumped on that tiny bit of hope. "Think, Scarlett. It could be the wooden stake I use to pierce Lilith's slimy heart."

Her eyes crossed as her spirit wavered. "A name...the angel..." she hiccupped. "...uh, assigned to escort your...mother home." The slurring became more pronounced.

Hot damn! Satisfaction slammed into me. Finally, some forward movement. "Tell me, Scarlett," I shouted. "Tell me the damn name."

Hiccup. "Sonya."

"More, Scarlett! I need more than a first name!"

"Jones."

"The wedding singer? Holy crap!" Stunned, I bolted from my chair and began pacing the kitchen. "Deena hired the hit woman? To sing at her wedding, and then when no one is looking, murder our mother? Oh, dear God, what has she done? And the better question is how am I going to stop Sonya Jones with doomsday closing in?" I grew more worried by the second. "Any suggestions?"

"There's   no...stopping   Sonya...Jones, girlfriend...she's the best...Heaven has."

I stopped in my tracks and turned to face her. "So this is it? Saturday's Mama's last day with us? There's nothing else for me to do?"

She shrugged her shoulders and gave me a lopsided smile. "As I've said...before, you can't stop a Death Angel. Especially...this one."

I moved to the counter and started a pot of coffee to sober her up. I now had a new direction to explore, and Scarlett was my only connection to Heaven's top assassin. I glanced at the clock. Ten o'clock. Hmm. Only twelve hours until our meeting with the wedding planner and Sonya Jones at the church. Twelve hours wasn't a lot of time to put together a plan, but that's all I had to work with, and I'd be damned if I'd stop now. I reached into the cabinet and pulled down two coffee mugs. It was gonna be a long night.

Chapter Nine
Earth Angel

The First Baptist Church of Whiskey Creek sat just off Main Street in the middle of town and occupied almost half a block. Surrounded by small shops and cafés and a lush green lawn, the red brick building stood out like the crown jewel it was designed to be. The Baptists were the largest denomination in town and extremely proud of their accomplishment.

Mama parked her Cadillac SUV beside a Ford F150 and an old yellow Volkswagen Beetle, and we all climbed out and headed inside. In the lobby, we heard female voices coming from the sanctuary, so we followed the sounds.

A tall, willowy brunette turned at our entrance. "Deena, darling, I'm so glad you're on time," the woman gushed in a high-pitched sugary tone. "Not long until the big day, and we have so much to finalize before the wedding rehearsal on Friday evening." She turned and laid a hand on the other woman's shoulder. "And this morning, Sonya will go through the songs you and Ryder picked out."

Deena brown eyes sparkled like diamonds. "Oh, Cheryl, do you think we'll get it all done? And I'm so excited to finally meet and hear the famed Sonya Jones."

Mama and Billie Jo sank down on the first-row

pew. Their faces wreathed in matching smiles. I, on the other hand, turned my psychic radar on full blast and swept my gaze over the woman standing next to Cheryl and felt, well, nothing. Not a twinge of the supernatural. Not a smidgen of the divine came from the petite, older woman in the Christmas red, fitted suit with a skirt just below the knees and matching pumps. Her vintage velvet pillbox hat, with a little fluff and feathers, sat atop freshly coffered silver-streaked ebony curls, and her chocolate brown eyes met mine with amusement.

She was more like Mrs. Santa Claus than Heaven's deadliest assassin. Scarlett had gotten it wrong. Dead wrong. I would bet my life on it. Sonya Jones was an angel all right—an earth angel. Sweet and angelical. The perfect Southern lady, and not prone to acts of violence. Satisfied with my conclusions, I turned my back on the woman and sat down on the pew next to Mama and Billie Jo.

Cheryl clasped her hands together. "However, before we get started there is some alarming news I need to share with you."

Deena's eyes went wide with alarm. "Oh, dear God, please not another problem."

Cheryl laid a soothing hand on Deena's arm. "Don't panic, but the bakery burned down early this morning."

"My wedding cake!" Deena let out a terrifying screech that had us on our feet. She burst into tears, and we bustled over to her side. Mama gathered her in her arms and started cooing like a turtledove. I looked up just in time to see Pastor Inman bust through the side door, his face twisted with horror.

"What's going on in here? I thought…no…I heard

a woman scream," he explained.

"Damn right, you did." Deena's flushed face matched her red lipstick. "It was me—my wedding cake went up in smoke!" She burst into fresh tears, and Mama drew her tight against her breast, and said, "Hush now, we'll get another cake for the wedding. Jolene will see to it." She gave me the eye over Deena's shoulder.

I bit my lower lip to keep a straight face. How the hell did Mama think I would be able to pull off such a stunt before Saturday? One couldn't order, and have delivered in six days, a three-layer wedding cake worth eating, not in this small town. We only had two bakeries, and one just went up in flames. However, I deemed it wise to keep my thoughts to myself. At least until Mama and I were alone.

Cheryl heaved a sigh. "This is all my fault, Deena. I should've said right away that I've lined up a cake tasting for one o'clock today. Al, over at Al's Baked Goods, said he can have the cake delivered on Saturday if you choose the flavor today. I'm doing everything in my power to make sure you have the perfect wedding. Trust me."

I struggled not to roll my eyes. Billie Jo looked doubtful, but like me, kept her opinions to herself. The less said, the better. We were all stressed out with the wedding preparations and Mama's particular predicament. Which reminded me...yep, Sonya Jones hadn't moved a muscle. Amusement still shone out of those perky brown eyes. I slid my gaze back to my sister.

Deena lifted her head. Her eyes met mine. Tears edged down her cheeks, streaking the perfect makeup.

"You're coming with me, right, Jolene? Ryder had to fly to Atlanta for business and to make travel arrangements for his parents. He won't be back until tomorrow night."

I nodded. "Of course. We'll all come."

Mama and Billie Jo both agreed, and she sighed in relief. "You're the best," she said and sank down on the front pew. Pastor Inman excused himself and disappeared back through the side door. With all eyes on her, Cheryl directed Sonya to take her place where the flower-draped trellis would be positioned for the ceremony and hit the play button on the portable CD player.

With a full piece orchestra providing the background, Sonya began to sing *Ave Maria*. Tears gathered in my eyes as I was swept away by the pure magic of her soprano voice and angelic expression. Beside me, Deena squeezed my hand and released a dreamy sigh as she allowed the music to sweep away her worries. She was getting married to the man she loved, and that was all that mattered. For me, the world remained balanced on my shoulders, and, in six days, unless I could stop it, my world would come crashing down.

****

As we stepped through the double glass doors of Al's Baked Goods, I did a quick radar sweep of the building for any troublemaking spirits, namely, Lilith and any of her hellish cohorts out for some fun at my expense. Thankfully, the place was clean of the undead, and Lilith had been absent in both body and spirit. Sonya Jones, I dismissed completely. She was too grandmotherly to be a threat to anyone.

A few people were waiting at the counter, and I recognized a long-time client placing an order for a dozen triple chocolate cupcakes and three dozen frosted sugar cookies. She waved at me when she exited the store with her young daughter, and the next customer in line gave his order to the girl in a white apron standing behind the pristine countertop.

The glass display case which ran almost the entire length of the room was filled with cakes, cookies, donuts, and every kind of sweet pastry to appease even the pickiest sweet tooth. Colorful posters of birthday, wedding, and special occasion cakes lined the pristine white walls. The timeworn wooden floors were dented and scuffed but polished clean. Café-styled tables topped with red and white checkered tablecloths had been strategically placed around the cozy room to avoid overcrowding. The place was a sensory overload with the aroma of pastries and baking bread filling the air. I inhaled a sweet-scented breath and imagined myself biting into a slice of fresh bread slathered with real butter.

Deena pointed to a corner table. "You guys have a seat, and I'll let the girl know we're here to see Al."

Billie Jo, Mama, and I did as instructed and settled down at the table. Billie Jo kept eyeing the glass display case with interest.

"Would you like me to fetch you something sweet, Billie Jo?" I started to rise, but she waved me down.

"That's why I agreed to come, Jolene." She patted her stomach. "For the baby. He's thrilled to taste a sampling of wedding cakes." She rubbed her hands together with anticipation.

I quirked a brow. "So you and Roddy have decided

it's a boy?"

"Of course, it's a boy." Mama reached over and patted Billie Jo's stomach. "Raleigh Tucker Hazard. A good solid Southern name for my grandson."

"What if it's a girl?" I teased. Lilith had predicted a boy, but I still wasn't trusting her to tell the truth about anything.

"It's not," Billie Jo said with confidence. "Call it intuition, but somehow I know I'm carrying a boy. Roddy and Lynette both want a *Georgia Bulldog* themed nursery since that's where Lynette is going after graduation, but I'd like a *Winnie the Pooh* themed room. Besides, he may not attend the University of Georgia like his sister."

"Bite your tongue," Mama said with a grin. "The *Dawgs* rule."

Deena halted any further discussion when she returned to the table and took her seat. She glanced down at her watch for about the tenth time since arriving. Immediately, Al Butterfield came rushing from the back room over to our table.

Smiling, he said in a deep baritone voice, "I'm so sorry to keep you waiting. We've been slammed since Twinkle Toes burned down this morning. But never mind, who is the bride-to-be in need of a wedding cake?"

I did a double take at the man, and his amazing, sexy voice, and nudged Mama who flanked me on one side.

Al Butterfield was bald, heavyset, and tall, about six-foot-three-inches with a large solitaire diamond earring in one droopy earlobe. He wore white…everything. Sparkling white pants, shirt, shoes, and jacket. The only thing missing was the clichéd baker's hat, and I briefly wondered if he had a platoon of baker elves stashed in the back because it appeared that he never lifted anything heavier than a wooden spoon.

"I'm the bride," Deena pronounced with a buttload of pride in her voice. "And these ladies are my mother and sisters."

Al's eyes settled on my chest. Oh, I should mention that in my hurry this morning, I'd thrown on a tight, long sleeve denim dress with a plunging V neckline that displayed my abundant cleavage. Mama shot him a hard look and cleared her throat.

Al flushed and swung his gaze back to Deena. "Can you tell me what you have in mind for your cake?"

"We decided to go with the traditional three-layer cake and would love your suggestions for the filling. My original cake had lemon curd and raspberry filling with a vanilla buttercream icing."

He bobbed his head eagerly. "That's an excellent choice and easy to replicate in the time frame. However, I do recommend you try the different flavor combinations I've prepared for you. My fall brides usually choose an autumnal theme such as apple cake or carrot cake with cream cheese frosting. Does this sound like something you would be interested in?"

"Sounds good to me," Billie Jo said. "I hope you have prepared something in chocolate."

Al glanced at Billie Jo, then back at Deena. "Most of my brides shy away from chocolate wedding cake this time of the year, but I can do a chocolate mousse filling with a white sponge cake and white chocolate ganache frosting."

Billie Jo's eyes gleamed, and I swear she licked her lips. "Please tell me you have one of those ready for us to taste."

A rush of endorphins flooded my bloodstream, and I laughed out loud at the adorable, gluttonous expression on her pixie face. Being pregnant is the only time in a woman's young life that she can eat whatever she wants and get away with it. And since weight had never been an issue for her, I relished the idea of her feeding her chocolate addiction at today's cake tasting. Just for my baby sister, and in spite of the season, I would cast my vote for a chocolate wedding cake.

Al nodded his head at Billie Jo. "Yes, I have included chocolate in my selections. I'll be back with the first sampling." He waited for Deena's nod of approval, then turned on his heel and scurried off in the direction of the swinging doors behind the display case.

Deena's frown deepened. "I understand your love of chocolate, Billie Jo, and I sympathize with your cravings. However, Ryder despises chocolate so we won't be having a chocolate wedding cake no matter what, understand?"

I felt a flash of irritation at Deena's hurtful tone, but quickly dashed it as Mama's expression instantly changed to one I remembered well from my childhood.

"I'll buy you a whole chocolate cake before we leave, sweetie pie," she said, patting Billie Jo's hand. "My grandson can have anything he wants." Here she turned and smiled at Deena. "And you can eat sour lemons to match your mood, my dear."

A wash of color suffused her face. "It's my wedding, Mama! I'm a teensy overwrought and snappy.

I'm sorry if I sound like a shrew."

My danger radar beeped out a stern warning just before the front door of the bakery opened, jingling the bells above it, and Lilith Lacewell strolled in looking like she just stepped off the pages of a fashion magazine. (I don't read them, but Deena leaves them lying around her office, and I've fingered through a time or two out of sheer boredom.) Lilith's dark eyes swept the room, then settled on us. A wide smile broke on her face, and I was instantly on my guard as she glided across the space between us.

"Well, glory be," she said, in a satisfied tone as she stood over our table. "Imagine running into you gals. I thought you'd be busy with last minute wedding preparations."

"That's exactly what we're doing," Deena replied with an expectant glance at the swinging doors. "A last-minute emergency with my wedding cake. Twinkle Toes Bakery burned down this morning. That's why we're here. Wedding cake tasting."

"How dreadful for you, my dear." The voice was sweet. Too sweet. I narrowed my eyes and zeroed in on the snake gazing at us through lazy half-closed lids. She was up to something for sure. Why else would she be here? Coincidence? Hardly. Lilith Lacewell was out for blood—Mama's blood and my soul. But she had another thing coming if she thought I was going down easy. No sirree. I'd fight till my last dying breath.

Which might be today. Taking no chances, I made the sign of the cross over my chest and ignored Mama's quizzical glance as my danger meter zapped me with another jolt of electricity as the vibrational frequency shifted north. A buzzing set up in my bones and my peripheral vision shimmered with pulsating silver light. I shook my head to dispel the odd sensation to no avail. The bell over the door jangled, and I glanced over as Sonya Jones pushed through the door and waved a cheery hello in our direction.

From the back room, Al swung through the swinging doors with a tray of wedding cake slices. He gave Lilith a quick glance, then placed a plate in front of Deena, Billie Jo, and Mama, before seemingly changing his mind and shifting the plate in front of me.

The atmosphere crackled as Billie Jo lifted a forkful of cake to her mouth.

Lilith's full lips thinned into a sneer. "Well, I'll leave you ladies to your tasting and run along back to the salon. So much to do before my opening," she intoned, as Deena dipped her fork into the sample.

Deena waved her off and slipped a bite of chocolate cake into her mouth. Billie Jo mumbled happily, and she took another bite. Her eyes rolled heavenward, and Mama and I exchanged a smile at her obvious delight. Mama tasted the cake on the only plate left and gave me a thumbs up, and I picked up my fork. Lilith's presence had unsettled me and stolen my appetite. Then add in Sonya's unexpected appearance, and I was perched on the edge of paranoia. However, for the sake of family unity and forestalling any drama from Deena, I scooped up a bite of chocolate cake onto my fork and hesitated as my mind replayed Al's odd behavior.

The slice of cake on the table before me had initially been placed in front of Mama, but Al, after a quick glance at Lilith, had shifted the plate over to me. Why? Was he in cahoots with the powers of evil? Or had the switch merely been a coincidence? The later was most likely true; however, I was taking no chances with my life. With a subtle move of hand that would be perceived as accidental, I swept the plate off the table and onto the floor.

Better safe than sorry was becoming my new life mantra.

Chapter Ten
Dixieland

After an hour of lively debate, Deena chose a naked apple cake with cream cheese frosting with a lemon citrus glaze, decorated with fresh apples and edible fall leaves for her wedding. Delighted with her choice, Al assured her it would be delivered and set up in the church reception hall at least two hours before the reception was scheduled to start. Since Cheryl was in charge of the event and would handle any problems, Deena agreed, and we left the bakery in a relatively good mood.

Billie Jo and I headed for our respective homes while Mama accompanied Deena for her final fitting at Gail's Formal Wear down the street from the salon. As I turned onto Love Avenue, I again questioned the wisdom of allowing Deena to watch over our sainted mother during this questionable time as visions of wedding day disasters danced in her head.

Chalk up one more reason why I'd never walk the matrimony mile again.

A quiver of movement in the front plate glass window caught my eye as I passed Dixieland Salon, and I hit the brakes and did an illegal U-turn on Love Avenue and zipped into the front parking space. The salon was closed on Mondays, and the cleaning crew usually finished by mid-morning. The place should be empty as employees weren't allowed on the premises after closing. Besides, it was tough enough to get them here on time when we opened Tuesday morning.

From my vehicle, I watched for any further sign of movement, and after ten minutes of nothing happening, I decided it had been a trick of the light and not an actual intruder. We'd had a break-in a couple years back which had resulted in Scarlett's demise, and I didn't want a repeat of that disaster on our heads. One death in my place of business was enough.

"Better safe than sorry," I murmured to myself, and with death on my mind I slipped from my car and unlocked the front door and stepped inside. Silence and the strong aroma of lemon Pine Sol wrapped itself around me while I made a quick tour of the salon and checked for any signs of disturbance.

The place sparkled like a new spring morning, and I found nothing out of order. Even the facial room held no surprises. Satisfied that it had indeed been a trick of the eye, I retraced my steps to the front door, and with one last glance over my shoulder, went outside and relocked the door.

As I returned to my car, my attention sharpened on the large sign proclaiming Lilith Lacewell's beauty shop's grand opening next week. Housed in the newly renovated Shacklefort building, the retro style immediately gave one an impression of 1960s easy, Southern lifestyle. The redbrick storefronts overlooked worn sidewalks with quaint, black antique lampposts and street signs. The city council had approved the black, square planters lined along the street with seasonal flowers and scrubs, and a wave of envy grabbed hold of me as I gauged the competition and her location.

Time for a little snooping on ole sulfur breath. My sleuthing antennae shot up in a snap.

From where I stood, I could see the closed sign on the door. Temptation gave me the go-ahead, so I crossed the street and stood in front of the plate glass window. Pressing my face against the glass, I peered inside. Hmmm, empty but for the gleaming oak floors and a few retail shelves.

Of course, I knew Lilith Lacewell's true motivation for being in Whiskey Creek, and it, sure enough, wasn't to open a viable business. She was here to collect a soul—mine or Mama's—and it didn't make a hill of beans to her which one.

Either way, she'd win.

Unless I could stop her.

Okay, so I know I've failed thus far in my quest to stop Hell's version of the Terminator, but I'm not the kind of woman who easily gives up on a task. Chalk it up to my background in cosmetology for that practical philosophy. Repetitive actions produce positive results, my teacher, Mrs. Butler, drilled into our heads daily through the 1500 hours to graduation.

"Checking out the competition?" my brother-in-law's voice asked from behind me, and I whipped around to face him.

"Never hurts to know your enemies' weaknesses," I replied, taking a visual tour of his person. Not in his usual work clothes. Dress slacks and shirt. Hmmm. Curious. "What brings you here, if I may ask?"

His gaze darted to the plate glass window, then back at me, then back to the glass. "I'm surprised to hear you say that, Jolene." He licked his lips. "I can't imagine anyone as sweet as Lilith Lacewell being anyone's enemy. She's new to town and in need of friends. Where's your Christian charity, sis?"

His uneasiness struck me as odd, and I zeroed my sleuthing periscope on his body language. Fidgety and defensive. Uh, huh. Speaks volumes. I narrowed my eyes and repeated the question, although I didn't really suspect Roddy of hanky-panky—he's not that kind of man—but Lilith Lacewell would use any means to bring me down, and right now, Roddy was a perfect stool pigeon. Ripe for the picking you might say.

"What brings you here, Roddy? I mean here at Lilith's salon?"

"He's here to see me."

I froze at the sound of Lilith's smooth purr behind my back, then did a perfect pirouette to face her. "Hands off, Lilith. Roddy is married to my sister." Although I managed to maintain a level tone, my fists clenched at my sides.

"That's enough, Jolene," Roddy barked. "This is a business meeting."

My eyes never left the she-devil's face. "The higher a monkey climbs, the more she shows her ass, Roddy."

"Are you insane?" He blew out a frustrated breath. "My God, I can't believe you just said that! You owe Miss Lacewell an apology."

"When pigs fly."

Lilith relaxed under my heated gaze and touched Roddy's sleeve with a manicured finger. I bristled with indignation but didn't act upon the inclination to wipe the pavement with her face when she said in a provocative voice, "Shall we go, Roddy...I mean, Mr. Hazard? I'm quite anxious to discuss my project with you."

"What project?" The question slipped out before I could stop myself.

Lilith's hand snaked out and wound itself around Roddy's arm. "Mr. Hazard has kindly agreed to take over my shop renovations."

I quirked a brow at Roddy. "Billie Jo said you were working on the baby's nursery."

Roddy's expression hinted at impatience. "The nursery can wait. Miss Lacewell has doubled my usual fee. And now if you will excuse us, we'll take off for our meeting." He turned to Lilith. "I'll meet you at my office in ten minutes?"

Lilith waved a hand in front of her face. "I'll see you there." She shot me a victorious smile before slinking off to a shiny, blue Cadillac convertible parked along the street and slid behind the wheel.

Roddy gave me a final look of disgust, then walked over to his work truck. The engine roared to life.

With my panties in a wad, I watched them drive away and reached for my cell phone to call Billie Jo when a melodious voice sang in my ear. *"I wish I was in the land of cotton, Ole times there are best forgotten; Look away, look away, look away, Dixieland."*

I slipped my cell phone back into the front pocket of my denim dress. "Okay, Scarlett, knock it off."

"In Dixieland, I'll take my stand."

"I'm not in the mood for childish games."

When several passer-byers gave me strange looks, I turned my back on them and stared into the empty shop and whispered, "I suppose there's a meaning behind the song?"

"Of course, *dar*-lin'." She giggled. "We need to

talk. Meet me inside."

"The door's locked, dingbat."

"I'll open the back door for you, *dingbat*!"

I waited until the sidewalk was clear of shoppers, then casually strolled around to the back of the building and counted the doors until I arrived at number ten. Tentatively, with one finger I touched the knob, half-expecting to get goosed by a shot of electricity. Nothing happened, yet, still, I paused to question the wisdom of entering the devil's domain.

The door swung inward of its own accord, and I glanced over my shoulder for any observers to my illegal entry. The alleyway was clear of pedestrians, so I eased in and closed the door. As the heavy, ominous silence of the empty shop embraced me, I took a few cautious steps from the back part of the shop toward the front, expecting Scarlett to materialize any second in front of me as was her customary habit.

She didn't, and for a split second, I froze in my tracks—paralyzed with uncertainty. From my peripheral vision, I detected fierce yellow eyes glowing from the shadows, and a cold tremor slid through my limbs.

"Okay, Scarlett, come out now, or I'm outta here," I whispered through stiff lips, my body tense and ready for any movement from anybody or anything. "And for all the rest of you guys, you should know that I'm wearing a cross." I lifted the diamond cross pendant snuggled between the girls and flashed it in front of me like a shield.

A sudden draft of hot wind whistled through the room, reminiscent of Lilith's foul breath, so close and oppressive, I bolted for the front room where late afternoon sunshine streamed through the plate glass window. Here the air felt lighter and less menacing.

And there was Scarlett, now dressed in traditional Scottish attire, complete with kilted skirt, ah, shortened to mini length, a black turtleneck pullover and boots, and a tartan shawl. She floated over to a lone ladder in the middle of the room and waved a gloved finger at me. "I wanted to tell you that I'm being dispatched to Scotland for the Christmas season, Jolene."

"And you couldn't tell me this outside?" I rubbed away the chill on my arms. "Why'd you make me come into the devil's lair for something as trivial as your holiday travel plans? It's creepy as hell in here. And what's up with the folk song? Definitely not your style."

She floated down like a gently flowing breeze to face me. "Oh, I don't know, Claiborne. It's just a song that's stuck in my mind. Nothing important. However, I wanted to say good luck and goodbye. I won't be back on this side of the Atlantic until New Year's."

"But what about Mama?"

"I just told you. I'm off to Scotland." She readjusted the tartan shawl.

"What about Lilith?"

"The Boss dispatched a team to take care of her."

"Where are they?"

"Hell if I know, Claiborne. I'm not on the team."

I clasped the cross in my fist and squeezed for some unknown reason. Good luck? Perhaps. Nothing else was working in my favor. "The seventeenth is six days away, Scarlett, and I'm no closer to stopping this injustice. Oh, and no way, Sonya Jones is the Grim Reaper. Mrs. Santa Claus, I'd believe, but not Heaven's assassin."

"Your belief isn't necessary, Jolene." She consulted a glitzy gold watch on her tiny wrist. "I really need to shove off now for Scotland. The Boss has me under supervision. I only stopped by to say goodbye and wish you a happy holiday. I'll check in with you after New Year."

"What if I have a problem?"

"Call the hunky detective in Wyoming," she drawled with distinct mockery and offered me a snide smile.

I didn't argue. No point. "Okay, go if you must, but remember the promise you made the other day."

"I made no promises, Claiborne, nor will I."

"Would you consider a short trip home for Deena's wedding? Please, Scarlett. You're family. Deena would say the same if she were here."

She blinked several times, then pulled a tissue from her glove and dabbed her eyes. "I'm family? Geez, Claiborne. You really know how to make a girl cry. Oh, pooh, what the heck. A few minutes away from the castle won't hurt. I'll be there."

With those last words, she walked through the front plate glass window and out of sight. Feeling the glowing eyes settle on me once more, I backtracked out the back door and around to the front, then sprinted across the street to Dixieland Salon—anxious to put some distance between me and Lilith's little shop of demons.

****

An unusual calm settled over Whiskey Creek for the remainder of the week. Roddy and his crew began work on my competitor's beauty shop across the street, and Billie Jo seemed cool with it, although I detected an undercurrent of tension in her voice when we spoke over the phone. For the sake of peace in the family, I let it drop but kept my psychic radar trained on Roddy for any sign of marital discontent.

Lilith Lacewell dropped out of sight. Not a peep.

Which did nothing to calm my nerves.

On Friday, I finished my appointments early so I could swing by the church and help Cheryl with the last of the decorations in the auditorium and reception hall. The hours passed quickly and without incident, and I was doubly relieved when Cheryl finally pronounced the wedding preparations were complete. So it seems like Deena *would* get her fairy-tale wedding and reception.

On Friday, as the rehearsal dinner wound down, I tried to be happy for her, but tomorrow was the seventeenth and Mama's last day among the living.

Chapter Eleven
Going to the Chapel

Deena's wedding day dawned bright and warm, and I rolled out of bed with nervous energy and a desperation that had my blood humming in my veins. My cell phone shrilled almost immediately, and I could see that Deena shared my prewedding jitters.

"Mornin' sis," I said when I hit the talk button. "Kind of early for the bride to be up and about."

"I could say the same for the Maid of Honor," she replied in a hushed tone. "Damn, Jolene, I'm happy and sad at the same time. I wish Ryder and I had eloped. I'm not sure I can make it down the aisle now. I'm bushed."

"No, you don't wish you'd eloped, trust me." I stumbled into the kitchen and hit the brew button on the coffee maker. "You've had fun planning this wedding, and you've spent a lot of quality time with Mama. Listen, Deena, there's something I need to tell you, but, first you have to promise not to freak out, okay?"

There was a pause on the other end. "I don't think I'm going to like what you're going to tell me, Jolene. Not today of all days. Can't it wait until tomorrow?"

"No, I'm afraid not, Deena. I should've told you before now, but I didn't want you to cancel your wedding."

"Oh dear God, what now?"

I inhaled a deep breath and exhaled slowly. "Don't freak out but Mama is scheduled to catch the long black train sometime today."

There was a silence and then a groan. "I wished I hadn't asked. And I hate to ask this, but are you saying Mama is…God, I can't even say it. On my wedding day?"

"Well I can, and yes, on your wedding day."

"How? Another accident?"

"Don't know, but Scarlett says that Sonya Jones is the angel assigned to bring her home."

"The wedding singer is the Angel of Death? I don't believe it."

"Neither do I. If anyone is an Angel of Death it's Lilith Lacewell."

"I'm going to cancel the ceremony. Ryder will understand when I explain the situation to him."

"No, you're not. I'll think of something. Mama's not going to die today, I promise."

"You're not God, Jolene."

"I know, but I've got to stop this injustice. Oh, I need to tell you something before I hang up."

She groaned loudly over the line, and I heard a long sigh of resignation. "Okay, give it to me straight."

"I invited Scarlett to the wedding."

"Well, for once I'm glad she's going to be there. She's helped us before; hopefully, she will again. Anything else before I have my first cup of coffee?"

"Yeah, one more thing. Hang in there, sis. Today, you're marrying your best friend and lover, and no matter what happens, you'll have him forever by your side." Sniffles sounded over the line.

"Thanks, Jolene; I needed to hear that this

morning. See you later at the salon."

I clicked off and poured a cup of steaming black coffee, added cream and sugar, and took my first sip. Tango jumped down from his perch on top of the refrigerator and wound around my ankles, yowling for his breakfast.

I fed the cat, lingered over toast and coffee, and watched the local TV station for an update for this afternoon's weather. Sunny and warm. A perfect November day for my sister's wedding.

A perfect day to die.

The unbidden words echoed through my mind, bringing a shudder down my chilled spine, and I fought back the impulse to call Bradford just to hear his calming voice. I fingered the phone lying inches away.

"Sam Bradford is your past," I reasoned aloud, pushing the phone across the table. "Today you will need all of your wits and abilities in keeping Mama alive and getting Deena happily married to her charming prince."

With those thoughts firmly planted in my mind, I cleaned the kitchen and dressed in comfortable slacks and a blouse for my hair appointment with Lizzie at the salon. At eleven, I scooted out the door and drove over to the shop and spied Deena and Mama's vehicles parked side by side in the rear parking lot.

Inside I found them seated in black leatherette stylist chairs surrounded by patrons and well-wishers vying for position to congratulate Deena and hug Mama's neck—one of the perks of living in a small, Southern community. Daddy waved from one of the reception chairs, and I blew him a kiss as I pushed through the women, all the while receiving my share of happy greetings. Mama appeared blissful and glowing with health, and for the hundredth time this morning, my spirits plummeted. Plastering on a wide smile, I pecked her on the cheek and moved on to Lizzie's stylist chair.

"Fine day for a weddin', Jolene," Mama beamed at me from her chair. "Maybe next year you and Preston will be tying the knot."

A chorus of high-pitched feminine agreements followed her not-so-subtle announcement, and I ignored the comments that followed and watched Lizzie in the mirror as she brushed out my long, frizzy hair.

"What are we thinking this morning?" Lizzie set down her brush and pulled out a box of bobby pins from her drawer. "A nice drape of sausage curls over one shoulder? Or would you like it falling down your back in a waterfall of curls?"

"Neither," I replied. "Do it back in a chignon and fasten in the sprigs of flowers that match my gown. The style and flowers will hide the singed portions I couldn't cut off." I pointed to several sprigs of dusty yellow and maroon silk flowers I'd placed on her workstation. "Keep it simple and no teasing. And light on the hairspray."

Thankfully, Lizzie followed my instructions, and thirty minutes later I was finished. Mama was under the dryer, so I stopped to check with Deena for any unfinished preparations that needed doing before the ceremony at two. If none, I would head home for a quick lunch before leaving for the church. We had two hours before the ceremony began, and the photographer wanted to take pictures in the sanctuary first.

"Crunch time, sis," I said as the stylist, Gail,

fastened a curl into place with a rhinestone bobby pin.

Deena glanced down at her watch. "I'm almost done. What do you think? Is it too much?" She gazed at her reflection in the mirror. A hopeful look flitted across her flushed face.

"No, it's perfect." I touched the glossy curls pinned into place with rhinestones. "You're going to be a beautiful bride, Deena. Now, is there anything I can do for you before I run to the house?"

"No, I just spoke with Cheryl, and everything is on schedule." She handed Gail a twenty dollar tip and grabbed her purse from the counter. "Billie Jo and Roddy will meet us at the church around twelve-thirty." She cast a glance over her shoulder. "What about Mama? She's not quite ready to leave. Is it safe to leave her here?"

I nodded. "Daddy's not going to let her out of his sight. Once they're finished here, they're heading straight over to the church. Not much can happen between here and the church in the next thirty minutes."

"Don't count on it, Jolene. Our family isn't known for having good luck. Are you positive I shouldn't cancel the ceremony?"

The worry in her voice had my eyes glued to her face. Stress lined every smile line on her pretty features, and I felt another pang deep in my gut. Yes, I was worried about Mama, but I could hardly confess my fears to her on her special day. And especially not here at the shop where gossip traveled faster than the speed of light. No, I had to erect a façade of confidence and certainty and pray my family made it through the day without suffering a tragedy. If I failed in saving Mama, then at least I would see that Deena was happily married and assured of a new beginning. With that in mind, I took her by the arm and steered her towards the rear exit. "Stop fretting, sis. Have I let you down, yet? No? Then, come on, let's get you married."

****

Fairy-tale weddings are just that—fairy tales—and if my memory serves me well, Cinderella didn't recover her lost glass slipper and bag the guy until the end of the story. Not only did she have to wait until the end for her HEA, but she had to endure dysfunctional family ties that continually threw a greased monkey wrench into her hastily made plans.

Well, that about sums up Deena's wedding in a nutshell. Dysfunctional family, check. Pumpkins, check. Mice, check. Fairy godmother, check. (Scarlett popped in garbed in a transparent concoction of glittering pink angel dust which left nothing to the imagination. Good thing I was the only one who could see her naked butt cheeks.) Magic, for sure. Throw in Heaven's assassin disguised as a grandmotherly singer, and you have one paranoid Maid of Honor walking down the aisle with the Pink Panther, my .38 special, tucked securely to my stocking encased thigh.

The spiritual equilibrium tilted off-kilter during the marriage ceremony. Ryder was just slipping the ring on Deena's finger when the energy attunement skittered far to the left. My ears popped with the drop in the barometric pressure, and I noticed Deena doing the same. Over my shoulder, I heard Daddy clear his throat and Mama's delicate cough. Scarlett, who perched invisibly atop the electronic organ, shot off into the air and circled the sanctuary like a buzzard before landing beside me with a whoosh that ruffled the hem of my maroon silk gown. I sneezed as a pink cloud settled over me.

"Ooohhh, something's up in the cosmos," she said with a twang. "I believe the long black train has pulled out of the station, Jolene. A sure sign that the Death Angel is gettin' ready to do her stuff. Sorry, but it looks like the end for your momma."

Adrenaline shot through my bloodstream, and I looked to the front pew where Mama and Daddy sat peacefully holding hands, their faces reflecting joy and total ignorance of the crisis unfolding in the invisible realm before them. This sounds crazy, but I swear to God, the deep-throated woo-woo of a locomotive sounded over Deena's "I do."

Now on high alert for any violence, I touched the gun strap under my gown, and I shifted my gaze to Sonya Jones standing beside the organ. Her cheery brown eyes caught mine, and she smiled as if she could read my thoughts. However she remained frozen in place, and I knew from yesterday's rehearsal her next song was coming up after the vows were completed.

From the third row back, I spied Diane Downey and a pack of hens from the Ladies Auxiliary gawking at the back of Mama's head like she was Medusa. No threat here. Only flapping jaws.

Midway down the aisle toward the back of the church sat Jimbo White and his wife, Caroline. The couple too had their hostile gaze penned on my parents, and another jolt of unease skittered down my back. Jimbo's head jerked around, and his blue eyes glowered into mine. Yep, the peanut farmer definitely had a huge chip resting on his shoulder. However, I had to ask if he genuinely posed a physical threat to Mama? I doubted it. Jimbo was all bark and no bite. And Caroline? The poor woman looked much older than the thirty-six years I knew her to be. Hell, the woman had a half-dozen school-age children at home and one of them Lynette's teenage years. No threat there.

Warm air blew in my ear. "Psst, Claiborne. I really need to shove off before the fireworks begin. The Boss warned me to stay away from you. If I'm caught here...well, its trouble, that's what."

I dared not answer with all eyes trained on the wedding party, so I lifted Deena's bouquet to cover my mouth from prying eyes and whispered, "Don't go yet, I may need you."

"I've fulfilled my obligations."

"Please stay for the reception."

A shot of hot breath tickled my ear. "I'm not feeling it."

The train whistle sounded closer. "Ten minutes," I pleaded.

"Ten minutes, Claiborne, then I'm off to Stirling Castle."

I lowered the bouquet as Pastor Inman pronounced Deena and Ryder husband and wife and presented the new couple to the congregation. With smiles wreathing their faces, they turned to face the guests, and I handed Deena her spray of fall flowers and took the best man's arm as we fell in line behind them. Scarlett hitched a ride on my shoulder.

As Deena and Ryder proceeded to the reception hall, I waited at the double doors for my parents, as well as Billie Jo and Roddy. My niece, Lynette, a brown-haired, green-eyed beauty, was a knockout in a dark, navy, blue silk, sheath, and I experienced a pang of jealousy at her youthful exuberance. She immediately withdrew her cell phone from her shoulder bag.

"Cool dress, Aunt Jolene," she said as she breached the door. "Where's Becky and Hannah? I didn't see them."

"They haven't returned from Israel," I answered, and linked my arm in hers. "She hated to miss the wedding, but this was the only time Jacob could get away for an extended visit. His parents were anxious to meet Hannah."

My daughter Rebecca, and son-in-law Jacob were due back in the States by Christmas, and I for one would be glad for their return. I missed my three-year-old granddaughter, Hannah, and planned to pull out all the stops for a huge Christmas celebration. One the entire family would never forget. That is if everything didn't go belly up.

But first, we had to get through today.

Together, we stepped outside into the warm, afternoon sunshine and mingled with all of the other guests meandering toward the reception hall. Diane and her gaggle of hens stood nearby chatting like a pack of hungry hyenas out for fresh game. They spied us coming and turned their backs—which was okay with me. After things settled down, I planned to speak with Mama about her finding new friends and possibly a new church home.

"I see the vultures are out in record numbers," Scarlett buzzed in my ear.

Nearby, Jimbo and his wife were engaged in a conversation with Mr. Brown, a local farmer and longtime member of the church. There were sidelong glances, quick appraisals directed at us, and I knew they were discussing my parents' abrupt reversal in selling the farm.

A flash of red caught my eye, and I turned to see Lilith Lacewell clinging to Preston's arm as they picked their way through the crowd.

"What the hell is she doing here?" I said aloud. "And with Preston? He said he couldn't get away from the hospital."

"She's an invited guest," Roddy replied in a candid voice. "And my new client so lower your voice, Jolene. I need the work."

Billie Jo reached out and caught my hand in hers. "I know how you feel, sis, but we need the money. Babies and college tuitions aren't cheap, and we couldn't turn her down." She was trying to look strong and unshakable, but I read the uncertainty in her eyes.

The appearance of Sonya Jones out of thin air stilled my reply. Again, the spiritual equilibrium shifted heavily to the left, and the earth beneath me shook. I closed my eyes and drew in a long breath.

"Jolene honey, open your eyes."

Stunned, to hear Granny Tucker's voice—a sure sign that trouble was fast approaching—I opened my eyes and swung my head in all directions. First at Sonya as she poised ten feet from Mama, her face wreathed in serenity. Then at Lilith, as she and Preston bore down upon us. Even from this distance, I could see the evil intent shining from those amethyst eyes. Holy crap. The moment I had been dreading was upon me. I tore my eyes from the Dragon Lady as a loud police siren shattered the quiet murmurings, and the screech of tires on pavement brought the guests to a standstill. All eyes turned to Main Street as a speeding car shot out of a side street and hurled toward us with the police cruiser hot on his six.

Gunshots peppered the police cruiser as it closed in on the speeding car. Guests screamed and scrambled for cover as more shots pierced the warm, autumn day, and ricocheted off street signs and buildings.

I dove for cover behind a boxwood bush and peered around the greenery for any sign of my family. A scary, chill gripped me as I spied Mama standing frozen in place and Daddy lying face down on the sidewalk—motionless. Billie Jo, with Roddy's body protecting her, huddled several feet from Daddy. Crouched behind the bush, I hitched my gown over my thigh and withdrew my gun from its holster for self-defense.

Bullets ricocheted off pavement close to Mama's feet, but she remained frozen in place. Screams and shouts erupted around her, yet failed to penetrate her paralyzed state, and I instantly knew this was the moment of her death. Or not.

My breath slowed to a trickle as reality slammed into me—the do or die moment—okay, I was wrong about everything. Especially about myself and the sacrifice I'm willing to make for my family. I guess subconsciously I've always known I wouldn't allow Heaven and Hell to play ping pong with Mama and me, so I guess today I'm going to die.

With my gun cradled in both hands, I scrambled from the bush and rushed to Mama's side as another gunshot rang out. I pushed her to the ground but not before a bullet slammed into my chest. There was a sickening sensation of falling, then nothing as I gave into the suffocating darkness that comes with death.

Chapter Twelve
All I Have to do is Dream

I opened my eyes to a surreal world, and it took a moment or two before I realized that I was floating above my body, which was all too still for my liking, in a hospital bed. From my position near the ceiling, I had a bird's eye view of the hospital room and nursing staff monitoring various machines and tubes attached to my body. The quiet of the room was broken only by the beeping heart monitor, and the whoosh, pause, whoosh of the ventilator.

A little freaked out by the scene below, I glanced down at my transparent hands and bare feet. "I must be dreaming."

"I warned you to stay out of Heaven's plans," Scarlett spoke up from her perch on the overhead light fixture by the bed. "This is the price of interference."

"So I'm dead?"

"Not yet, but soon." She joined me on the ceiling. "I have it on good authority that your accommodations in Purgatory are being readied as we speak."

I fingered a thin, silver string attached to my side just below my heart. It twanged as I stroked the smooth surface. "What's this?"

"Your lifeline."

"I believe I'm going to need more of an explanation, Scarlett."

"It keeps you attached to your body."

"Whatever for if I'm destined to die?"

"Your spirit and body must stay attached until Saint Peter pulls the plug."

I zipped down to stand beside the bed and saw the thin, silver line attached directly to my body's heart. A nurse adjusting one of the machines passed through me as if I were a breath of air. I shivered as I encountered her living energy. It stung like a bee sting, and I zipped back up to rejoin Scarlett.

"How long do I have?" I watched the nurse add another IV bag to the others.

"God only knows."

"Will I get to tell my family goodbye?"

"Since you broke the rules, I'm pretty confident the answer is no."

"Well, that sucks."

"Yeah, well, we rule-breakers get a bad rap."

"I did it for a good purpose," I reasoned. "Shouldn't I get points for that?"

"You'll find out at your trial, but I wouldn't count on it."

A waft of antiseptic tickled my nose. "I hope my stay isn't very long. It stinks in here."

"I wouldn't be so anxious to leave if I were you," Scarlett said gravely. "Bein' dead ain't all I've cracked it up to be. It's all work and no play."

I gave her the once-over. "What are you doing here? I thought you had to be on your way to Scotland?"

"I told you there'd be consequences for my interference. The Boss grounded me when that snitch Sonya Jones reported back to headquarters."

"Grounded? What does that mean?"

"It means I'm stuck here with you until my probation hearing for bailing out on my duties in Scotland. Damn. I knew I should've skipped the wedding."

The sound of hushed voices halted our conversation, and I was surprised to see my parents walk up to the bed. Daddy reached for my hand, and Mama smoothed back a long lock of hair that had fallen across my face.

Both my parents were crying. I zipped down from the ceiling to stand at the headboard where I could see and hear them better.

"Jolene, can you squeeze my hand, honey?"

Daddy's broken voice barely registered above the noisy machines. I willed my hand to move, but it remained motionless.

"The rest of the family is waiting to see you." Mama sniffled and withdrew a tissue from her purse. "Deena and Ryder are here, and Billie Jo and Roddy. Lynette is too broken up, so she's not here. I haven't called Becky yet, but I will as soon as we know your prognosis."

She broke down then, and Daddy dropped my hand to rush around the bed to her side. Taking her hand in his, he gently steered her out of the ICU. Once they'd gone, I rejoined Scarlett.

"There has to be some way to reverse this present crisis," I pointed out. "Think Scarlett. Is there some way your boss will hear me out?"

"That's the purpose of your trial. To hear your motivation behind your actions, but I wouldn't get my hopes up, Claiborne. Rarely does the Council of Noble

Purposes committee change their minds once a person is on the list."

"But I wasn't on the list."

"You are now." She shook her head, sending angel dust falling only to disappear like melting snowflakes. "And not only did you alter Heaven's plans, but you also drug me into your mess. Now I'm in a buttload of trouble."

Shame and remorse washed over me for my rash actions. "Geez, Scarlett, I'm sorry, but I couldn't let Mama die. She's the glue that holds us together. If I hadn't acted, Mama would be the one down there, or worse, dead."

"She's supposed to be, Jolene. That was Heaven's plan, but I warned you and now what's done is done, and the past can't be undone. Let's peek in on the doctor's conference with your family."

"Can I do that?" I lifted the silver thread and pointed downward. "I mean, I'm connected to, uh, you know."

She chuckled. "Yeah, you can do that. Come on, let's eavesdrop."

"Wait, I need to change." I followed her to the glass door separating my room from the nurses' desk. "This hospital gown doesn't have a back, and my backside is exposed. It's cold, and I'm barefoot, and you know how I hate bare feet."

"Nothing to be done about it. You're in limbo."

"You mean I'm stuck with this getup?"

"Yep, just as I'm stuck with you."

With the back of my gown clutched in one hand, I followed Scarlett out of the ICU double doors and into the waiting room where my family, still in their

121

wedding finery, sat bunched together in the corner of the room in chairs and on a small sofa. Deena looked ready to collapse into Ryder's arms, and Billie Jo's makeup-streaked face reflected her distraught state. I floated over to her and placed a hand on her stomach and whispered a heartfelt plea for her to go home and rest. For the baby, I added. She, of course, didn't react to my presence. However, Deena did. The moment I wafted through the door behind Scarlett, her huge brown eyes grew round as saucers and surveyed the room with interest. Her reaction confirmed my suspicions: Deena was a sensitive—a psychic in training.

She was my closest link to the living. If I could somehow communicate with her, I could get a comforting message through to my family assuring them I was fine on the Other Side and not to worry. Excited at the prospect, I zipped back to Scarlett who was circling the young, handsome doctor entering the room.

"How do I communicate with the living, Scarlett?" I gushed. "Deena's aware of our presence. I need to get a message to her. Tell her I'm okay. She can then tell my family before I move on."

Scarlett reached out and cupped the man's buttocks. "Hmmm, tight as steel. See, this is what I meant when I said that you shouldn't be so anxious to leave, Jolene. You can't do this in Heaven. No sir, the best kind of pleasure is forbidden up there."

"Forget sex for one minute, Scarlett. I need your help."

She lifted a hand and smoothed back a tendril of bronze hair that had escaped the ponytail. "I heard you,

Claiborne, but communicating with the living is strictly forbidden. The die has been cast. The writing is on the wall. Now let's listen in on the conversation. This should be interesting."

I started to protest, but Mama's frightened words slammed into me. "You want us to do what? No. Tell him, Harland. We're not pulling the plug."

Deena's face blanched. "Oh dear, God, this can't be happening. Please say there's some hope, Dr. Moore."

Billie Jo broke down in tears, and Roddy tightened his arm around her. "We're going home for a bit," he said. "Billie Jo needs to rest, and I need to check up on Lynette."

"Please don't do anything yet," Billie Jo said explosively. "Give Jolene time to come back to us. You don't know her. She's a survivor."

Daddy enveloped her in his arms. "We're not doin' anythin' before we get a second opinion, sweetie. Go home with your husband. You need to think about the baby now. We'll call if there's any change."

Dr. Moore excused himself, and Roddy steered Billie Jo out of the ICU waiting room. Ryder turned to Deena. "Honey, let's go home and change into more comfortable clothes. We need to swing by Jolene's house and feed the cat. Plus, I need to check on my parents. Mother is still so weak. We'll be back in an hour or two, I promise."

"I'm staying here," Deena protested in a broken voice. "I can't leave her. Not yet."

Daddy reached out and caught her hand in his. "Go on with your husband. You're exhausted and need some rest. Your momma and I will be here. We'll go home for a few hours after you and Ryder get back. We can take turns. All but Billie Jo. She needs to keep off her feet for the baby's sake."

"Good luck with that," Mama muttered. "Billie Jo is stubborn just like Jolene. She's gonna buck like a Mustang if we try to keep her away."

A sudden tug on the silver thread had me hurling back to the tiny cubicle where my body lay connected to life-sustaining machines, and I stared in surprise at Preston who had pulled a chair beside my bed and was stroking my hand.

"I don't know how to say goodbye," he was saying. "I don't want to say goodbye, Jolene. The doctors don't have any hope for your recovery, but they don't know you like I do. Fight, Jolene. Fight with everything you've got because it's going to take a miracle to bring you back."

I willed my hand to move in his, but it refused to obey. Repeatedly, I wished my body to flinch or twitch with life. Nothing.

Preston stood and leaned over the bed and kissed my cheek. "I'll stop by later tonight and check on you before I go home. I saw your parents in the waiting room so I'll check on them before I see my next patient." After one last peck on the cheek, he left.

Scarlett joined me on the ceiling. "I think the end is coming soon. Don't worry, you've been through the worst of it. The rest is a piece of cake. Trust me."

Not encouraged by her words, and a little depressed at the thought of death, I drifted over to the bed and tried to slip back inside my body to no avail. "Why isn't this working?" I asked Scarlett, frustrated at my failed attempts. "My body keeps spitting me out."

She cocked her head to the side and appeared to be listening to something or someone. I heard nothing but a continuous ringing in my ears. Finally, she turned to me with a somber expression and said, "The Boss is on his way down here. This is bad, Claiborne. The Boss never leaves his post at the Pearly Gates. I warned you to stay out of Heaven's business, but no, you had to go and interfere." She flittered about the room like a drunk butterfly. "And not only you, Claiborne. Me. I'm on his shit list too." She folded herself into a speck in the corner wall.

I only had time to grasp the back of my hospital gown closed before a shrill trumpet blast echoed through the glass-enclosed room, and a burst of brilliant angel wings filled the space. Sizzling cosmic energy filled me with Heaven's fire, and I turned around to face The Boss.

Chapter Thirteen
Blue Suede Shoes

"Well, young lady, what do you have to say for yourself?"

I clutched the back of my gown tighter and smothered back a giggle as my gaze swept over the chubby florid-faced, elderly gentleman with fiery red hair and handlebar mustache. He wore a blue pin-striped suit with a high white collar and blue necktie. Naturally, I glanced down to check out his shoes, and let out an audible gasp at the sight of the most beautiful pair of blue suede shoes with silver buckles I'd ever seen.

My eyes traveled up the length of him to his smiling face. "Those shoes are to die for! I once had a pair of blue suede high heels."

He quirked a brow. "I remember the incident well. You ruined them in a fight with an old man as I recall. Rode him like a bronc buster and received a broken nose for your effort. Yes, dried blood isn't easily removed from suede."

I flushed with embarrassment. "Theo had it coming when he punched Daddy. I couldn't stand by and watch."

Penetrating green eyes seemed to look into my soul. "You're a regular busybody where your family is concerned. Your impulsiveness has landed you in trouble many times over the years, young lady." A tablet materialized in his hands, and he skimmed down the screen with one finger. "Hmmm, yes, here you are. Jolene Tucker Claiborne." His gaze lifted from the screen. "A habitual violator across the board." He clicked his tongue several times like Mama used to do when one of us girls crossed the line of accepted feminine behavior. "And now this infraction. Very serious indeed, and I'm not sure the lesson I have in mind will keep you on the straight and narrow."

Uncertain now, I shot a worried glance at Scarlett hugging the corner ceiling. Her face looked pinched, and waves of anxiety poured off her like water from a busted spicket.

"I wouldn't count on her for any help," the Boss said in a dry voice. "She's been nothing but trouble since her arrival in the Golden City, and I've been entertaining the idea of drafting her into the Peace Corps. They're short-staffed and spread thin, but I believe I have a better idea. Kill two birds with one stone, you might say." He chuckled. "Yeah, this is going to be something to watch from above." He crooked a finger at her. "Please join us, Miss Scarlett. And properly clothe yourself. Emissaries from Heaven must reflect purity and perfection. You know the rules!"

Back in her librarian duds, Scarlett drifted down from the corner ceiling to settle beside me, rebellion lined her face, and I doubted Heaven would ever put a bridle on her wild spirit. Scarlett was a true born and bred Southerner just like all the rest of us rednecks south of the Mason Dixon line. Like Daddy says, "You can't tame the wind, just redirect it."

He beamed at her. "That's much better, my dear. For the duration of your stay here on Earth, you will remain in that approved attire. And don't entertain the idea of pulling a fast one. I will be watching."

In the background, a nurse entered my room with a fresh IV bag in hand. Ignorant of the heavenly invaders, she proceeded to replace the empty container with a full one.

The Boss continued in his dry tone, "I have decided, and the Council of Noble Purposes have approved my plan, that you, Jolene Claiborne, deserve a second chance at life. Although you're headstrong and impulsive and love to dabble in sin, your intentions are good and honest, just misdirected. If you succeed in winning another chance in the physical realm, you must promise to give up your promiscuous ways. Simply unacceptable. Every dog should have a few fleas, indeed."

"You heard that?" My voice quivered with embarrassment and indignation. "Geez, isn't anything private anymore?"

He was referring to the morning Mama had walked uninvited into my bedroom. In anticipation of a little bedroom fun with Preston, I was butt naked and spread out invitingly upon the bed. And then, well, Preston arrived with pistols shooting, and moments later, Bradford. Boy, was that a morning to remember! (I disclosed all the details in another story.)

The handlebar mustache quivered. "That is not up for discussion, young lady. I'm here to offer you a fair proposition. Accept it, or you're off to Purgatory until your trial."

Fair proposition? What was this—let's make a

deal? Choose door number one and win a chance to walk out of this hospital alive or door number two complete with iron bars and guards? My answer was swift. "Life or death. Geez, so many tough choices an almost dead girl must make." I hope I didn't sound defensive, but damn, this was a no-brainer.

Scarlett punched me in the ribs. "Don't be a fool, girlfriend. Saint Peter is the Boss, and you never smart-talk the Boss. First lesson of Heaven."

I gazed at her with complete understanding, nodded, and then addressed the Boss. "Ah, I apologize for my rash tongue, sir. It won't happen again, I promise. And I accept your proposition." I tried to look contrite. A first, believe me. I'm naturally rebellious and fidgety in stressful situations. And he was making me antsy.

He wagged an admonishing finger. "I haven't proposed it yet, young lady." He scrolled down his tablet. "Okay. As you know, Lilith, the wind spirit, has recently taken up residence here in Whiskey Creek under the guise of a lovely young woman."

My gut bottomed out, but I nodded politely. "Yes, sir. She's opening a beauty shop across the street from my salon. She's a redhead, like you. Bossy, too."

He looked pained at the comparison. "Completely irrelevant, young lady." He pursed his lips with disapproval. "You must learn to hold your tongue if you wish to complete this task to my satisfaction. There is much at stake. Not only for you but for Whiskey Creek. This undertaking calls for discipline and courage."

"Just what is it you want me to do?" I asked cautiously and pointed to my lifeless body on the bed. "I'm not exactly in tiptop shape, if you get my drift."

"It won't be easy." His nod was empathic.

"It never is," I reflected in a neutral tone.

"Love is your only defense." He looked troubled.

"Love? What's love got to do with it? What is it you want me to do?" I repeated, a tad irritated at the delay. Scarlett pinched me hard on my upper arm just like Mama. I pinched her back.

"Love conquers all," he rumbled, his upturned handlebar mustache quivered like a bowl of jelly. "Hate cannot stand up to love. God is love. It is your only weapon against Lilith."

"I'm pretty sure I'm not grasping the idea," I told him. "Lilith is a fire-breathing she-demon with bad breath, and I'm gonna need more than love to drive her out of town. That is what you're driving at, right? For me to get rid of Lilith? No, can do. Isn't there something else because I'm fairly certain I'm not the loving type."

Saint Pete shook his head. "Getting rid of Lilith is beyond your capabilities, young lady. That's where Scarlett comes in. She was repeatedly warned to remain neutral where the list was concerned. She chose to ignore the rules, and instead passed along vital information which caused this present situation with you. So, as punishment for disobedience, she's banished from Heaven until further notice. You two make a good team, so I'm sure this task will prove to be a simple one. Simply said, I want Lilith driven from my jurisdiction, and you two are going to see to her departure. You have seven days to work your magic. Understood?"

Not really having a choice, we both gave a perfunctorily nod.

z"Excellent. Now for the rules." He cocked a bushy red eyebrow and eyed us both. Seemingly satisfied with our mutual acceptance, he cleared his throat, and from the inner pocket of his pin-striped suit, he withdrew a rolled piece of paper tied with a thin red ribbon. Unrolling it, he smoothed it out and handed it over to me. The list, printed in black calligraphy on yellow parchment, was entitled:

RULES OF ENEMY ENGAGEMENT IN THE PHYSICAL REALM

1. Keep to the shadows.

2. Avoid the public domain.

3. Do not consort with departed souls.

4. Avoid the living, especially psychics and mediums.

5. Maintain acceptable language. No cussing or slang words.

6. Work behind the scenes without making your presence known.

7. Keep the commandments.

8. Practice the Golden Rule.

9. Make every effort not to upset earthly creatures. Cats are the exception.

10. Do not engage in any sexual activities with humans.

I scanned it a second time, then handed it over to Scarlett to study. I had a few questions and demands of my own for Saint Pete. I picked up the silver thread attached to my side and asked, "Do I have to lug this thing around everywhere I go?"

"I'm afraid so. Your body and soul must stay attached. Lose that, and your earthly body dies."

Check. Protect silver thread lifeline at all cost.

"I would like a change of clothes." I was polite but firm. "This ensemble doesn't offer much protection against the elements. I'm sure you would agree with me that it isn't very heavenly for my backside to be exposed, and I can hardly complete my task to your satisfaction with one hand." I flashed my one free hand. "And a pair of shoes, please," I added for effect. "Oh, and one more thing, one of those big swords of light the angels carry would surely help us out."

He studied me intently. "I can see where your present state of undress might cause problems, so I believe appropriate attire is in order." He snapped his fingers, and I was instantly clothed in a floor-length, shimmering gown of white with matching slippers.

"Uh, this is nice, but not what I had in mind, thank you," I said amiably. "It's okay where you come from, but here in the South we prefer a good pair of sturdy jeans, a flannel shirt, and snake-proof boots."

"Since when?" Scarlett piped up in a snide voice beside me. "I've never seen you in anything but heels. Including boots. And you and I both know that you wouldn't be caught dead in snake-proof boots."

"That's right, I wouldn't, but I'm not dead yet, so I'll take the chance with the boots. I aim to win this battle, and I can't do it in heels." I raked my eyes down her priggish attire. "Or in that silly getup."

"I agree." Saint Pete snapped his fingers, and Scarlett and I were twin models for Bass Pro Shops. Snake-proof boots and all. Even my frizzy hair was twisted into a tidy knot at the back of my neck. Neat.

I patted my denim-covered bottom. "Wow, thanks, Saint Pete. This is warm and comfy. Right, Scarlett?"

Her stormy gaze swept down her body. "Thanks to you, I don't seem to have a voice in this matter, Claiborne. You might be surprised to learn that there is a limit to my sartorial sacrifice. Even for you."

Saint Pete hit the off button on his tablet. "Well, I believe I've covered everything. You both know the rules." He pointed a finger heavenward. "Remember I'll be watching."

"Wait!" I held up a hand to stop him. "What about my sword?"

"Denied. You're not licensed to carry." Again, another loud trumpet blasted, and he was gone.

I turned to Scarlett. "Okay, the first thing we have to do is establish our headquarters."

She planted her hands on her hips. "What's wrong with this place?"

"Well, for one thing, there's too much traffic." As soon as the words were out of my mouth, another nurse pushed through the glass doors.

A smile cracked the corner of her full lips. "I know just the place."

I gave a nod of approval. "Where else but Dixieland Salon?"

Chapter Fourteen
Shake, Rattle and Roll

Being almost dead has many perks. The first, being able to soar through the night sky like an eagle. The second, being able to waltz through walls and dive through ceilings without a peep of sound. The flight over from the hospital was a blast. Against the midnight sky, a full moon casts an incandescent glow over the sleeping town, and millions of twinkling stars flung out across the horizon like pebbles hurled by a mighty hand.

Innocent joy exploded through me as I zipped past Scarlett over city hall, the silver thread trailing behind me like an airplane contrail. "I'll race you to the salon," I yelled as I did several acrobatic loop-de-loops and plunged into a deep dive toward Main Street.

"Woo-wee." I skimmed along the pavement with my arms spread wide. Ahead of me, nestled among other small boutiques and cafés on Love Avenue, was Dixieland Salon, and I zoomed past with a joyful twist and looped around the building and dropped through the ceiling into the facial room.

Scarlett lounged back on the flower print chintz loveseat with lovely matching pillows. She shielded a yawn with the back of her hand. "I took a shortcut through the cemetery. Now, if you would be so kind as to settle down, I need my beauty sleep."

"Sleep?" I asked incredulously. "My life hangs in the balance, and you want to sleep?" I kicked the loveseat. "Get up. We need to put together a plan."

"I plan to sleep like the dead." She closed her eyes and released a heavy sigh.

Seeing I was on my own until morning, and too keyed up to remain still, I drifted out the door and into the hallway and down to the reception area where I drifted from station to station, allowing the familiar to comfort me. At my station, I plopped down on my black leatherette chair and stared into the large mirror as I'd done hundreds of times before.

My image was clear in the reflecting surface. Huge brown eyes in a pale heart-shaped face stared back at me. The mouth drooped a little at the corners, and I wondered if a short rocket ride out to the farm might perk me up a bit and ignite my brain cells. It was worth a try as I'd had no luck in dreaming up a worthy plan to send Lilith on her way.

Seven days.

Not much time. After that, Saint Pete would pull the plug.

That sobering thought sent me shooting through the roof and into the night sky. I headed south to my parent's farm on the outskirts of town. As I passed quiet streets and dark houses, I focused my thoughts on all the past Sunday school lessons I'd learned through my childhood. Surely there had to be a nugget of gold hidden somewhere in the thousands of hours of Bible study that I could use against Lilith.

Yet I could think of nothing but the beauty of the South Georgia autumn countryside bathed in the glorious light of the moon.

On the outskirts of town, I followed pasturelands and fields of beans and turnips and carrots. The scent of freshly turned dirt mingled with cow patties and pig farms to remind me of my childhood spent out here on the peanut farm. At the General Store, I turned eastward and followed the highway until I saw the flashing intersection light. At the light, I turned left onto Nelms Road and made a sharp right on See More Lane.

Several miles more and I would be home. When I streaked into the dirt driveway, a lone light shone in the kitchen window like a welcoming beacon. In the distance, I heard a train whistle and closer, the faint stirring of oak leaves rattling in the rising breeze. Warm and comfortable in my red flannel shirt and jeans, I circled the house with caution—not wanting to stir up the barn cats. If they sensed my presence, they'd set up a holler, and if my parents were home, I didn't want to disturb their rest with my arrival.

Being careful not to break any of the rules, Saint Pete had put forth, I floated to the front porch and paused just outside the front door. Silence, but for the usual snorts and pawing sounds from the barn, wrapped around me, and I drifted inside. In the foyer, I gazed lovingly at the family photos lining the wallpapered walls. Mama and Daddy's wedding photo taken in the old white clapboard church down the road. Billie Jo holding Lynette with Roddy beaming by her side. Deena and her two children, Bo and Summer. Me and Becky. Becky and Jacob. Hannah. 4-H photos. Fair Queen. Pecan pie contest. Harvest balls. Weddings. Birthdays. Graduations. They were all there. Each one in their special place on the wall. And in the middle—Grandpa and Grandma Tucker.

So many wonderful memories of my family. A stab of fear replaced the fuzzy, warm feeling, and I drifted over to the recent group photo my sisters, and I had gifted to our parents. If I failed my given task, I would never again interact with them. Never feel their arms around me. Or hear their laughter or wipe away their tears. I would never play with my granddaughter, Hannah.

So many what if's and what-could-have-been's. So many lost opportunities allowed to slip away. So much wasted time. So many lost chances at love. Bradford came to mind, and I brushed away a tear. He was my greatest loss of all.

From the kitchen, I heard the soft murmur of Daddy's voice, and I approached with extreme caution to see him sitting in his usual spot at the corner table with his Bible opened before him. He didn't lift his head as I wafted closer but continued murmuring in an urgent voice. I heard my name burst out in a painful whisper, and I realized he was praying for my recovery.

Tears dripped from his face to land on the crinkled pages spread before him. Before I could check my reaction, I reached out to comfort him and laid my hand upon his head. He stilled under my touch and released a tired sigh.

"Ah, Jolene honey, I don't know what to do. The doctors will only give you a few more days before they make us take you off life support or move you to another facility. Preston recommended a Dr. Peter O'Brien for a second opinion. If he can't help you, your momma and I are thinking of bringing you home here to the farm to care for you ourselves. If you can hear me, please come back to us, honey. I called Becky, and she and Jacob are catching the next flight home. I need you to hang on, baby. Give us a little more time to figure this out."

Tears began to flow again, and I felt another pang of remorse, knowing I had made a big mistake in coming here. Waves of crushing emotion poured over me as his sobs filled the kitchen. Feeling my spirits plunge, I drifted out of the kitchen and down the hall to my parent's bedroom. One last look at Mama and I'd be on my way back to the salon to wake Scarlett for an all-night planning session. She could catch up on beauty sleep after I was back on terra firma and among the living. We had a succubus to round up and escort out of town. Pronto!

Thankfully, Mama was asleep—albeit a restless slumber. Satisfied that all was well with my parents, I shot through the ceiling and headed back to Dixieland Salon at top speed. I was dropping through the roof of the facial room when a strong pull on my silver lifeline had me whirling backward through the night sky until I crashed back into my room in the ICU.

Dizzy from the wild ride, I gripped the sidebars of the hospital bed until my eyes settled back in my head.

"My, my, my. How the mighty have fallen."

Shock stole my voice as I turned to face my enemy. Lilith had shed her human form, and the Beast of the facial room rose from her crouched position to stretch long, leathery wings. Her lips stretched open, and her jagged teeth clicked and gnashed as she hissed a sulfurous giggle. "I told you not to fuck with me." The tip of her wing drew across my physical body in a long caress.

My heart rate skyrocketed. The heart monitor

connected to my body let out a warning shrill, and seconds later, a male nurse rushed through the door and stopped cold. He wrinkled his nose as if he could smell the foul breath of my visitor, and seeing nothing, rushed over to my bed.

"What brings you here?" I finally asked in a hushed voice. For the life of me, I couldn't shake off the fear gripping me at the slimy creature's blatant appearance in my hospital room. The heart monitor continued to squeal out a warning.

Lilith's eyes were so red they glowed. "To admire my handiwork."

"Okay, so now that you have, you can leave and never return."

"I'm going, but not before I enlighten you to my next target of interest."

I fought nausea. "Another target? I thought you wanted only me."

Lilith laughed puffs of nasty red and yellow stinky smoke. "Ah, Jolene, you've been such a delightful playmate. It's a shame I must move on, but someone else has captured my eye."

The nurse lifted his head and sniffed the air. He looked around, frowned, and then scurried from the room.

"So you're leaving Whiskey Creek?" A ray of hope laced my voice.

"As soon as I've enticed my target of interest to come with me."

"So you no longer have any interest in my mother?"

"I never had any interest in Annie Mae." Leathery wings beat against the glass walls making a soft whooshing sound. "Besides, I've found a more interesting plaything," she purred as the slimy creature began a slow transformation back into human form. "I've become attached to a man, Jolene. An extremely handsome man. One I want to play with. And, funny thing, I believe he's attracted to me." The transformation was complete, and her stunning amethyst eyes glittered with triumph.

"Roddy," I replied flatly, numb with fear. "Dear God, you're after Billie Jo's husband." I couldn't stop the tears from coming to my eyes.

Lilith caressed her breasts and sides with manicured hands. "Yes, my dear, Jolene. Soon he and I will taste the forbidden fruit, and he'll be lost to Billie Jo. Once I have a man, he's mine forever." She walked over to the ventilator machine. "Don't be a fool, Jolene. I know what you're thinking. You can't stop me, but I can stop you. Time for you to dance with the devil." With those words, she pressed a button, and another shrill alarm sounded as the ventilator shut down.

****

Traveling down the long tunnel toward the brilliant light didn't take long, and when I stepped out of the opening onto a green carpet of lush grass, I could hear the faint strains of Southern rock music coming from beyond the black wrought iron gates at the top of the white stone steps before me. The ornate sign above the gates proclaimed in black block letters that I'd landed just outside of Heaven. As I stood there on the bottom step, I heard the woo-woo of a locomotive, and a few seconds later it came into view from the distant fluffy pink and gold clouds dotting the clear blue sky. Fascinated, I watched it circle overhead and disappear behind a line of trees behind the fence that stretched as far as the eye could see.

Evidently, Heaven was a gated community, and I was reminded of the Westgate Country Club off Old Dalton Road back home in Whiskey Creek. Admittance to the ritzy social establishment was strictly monitored, and only the city's elite crossed those restricted doors. Did the same rules apply here? If so, I was positively out.

Feeling a tad warm in the brilliant sunshine, I glanced down at my jeans and flannel shirt and snake boots. Definitely inappropriate attire up here. I waved my hands in front of my face to create a breeze and climbed the steps to the top. Through the gates, I glimpsed a golden cobblestone road which meandered through the meadow of wildflowers toward the towering green mountains. I tested the gate and found it unlocked. The heavy gate squealed a protest as I pushed it open and stood on the threshold, uncertain of what lay ahead and if I should enter therein.

Surely, this wasn't the main entrance into the Golden City in the sky? Not an angel or celestial citizen within sight, and I'd always been led to believe that our deceased loved ones would be waiting at the gates to welcome us in.

No one waited for me. Nada. Not even Grandpa and Granny Tucker who I was most anxious to see.

Which led me to believe that I wasn't expected.

I could follow the cobblestone road.

It was, after all, the only way to find someone to give me directions back to the living. I had to get home and save Roddy from Lilith's seducing demonic wiles. Billie Jo's marriage depended on me finding my way back to Whiskey Creek, and for that, I would need the help of the supernatural kind.

Saint Pete was in there—somewhere just over the mountain peaks awash with golden light and smelling of the Texas Bluebonnets in spring. I hurried forward even though I had no clue what to expect of this adventure, and didn't even know if I was on the right path.

A light sweat peppered my upper lip and forehead by the time I reached the edge of the meadow, and I stopped to roll up my sleeves and remove the cumbersome snake boots. I wasn't completely barefoot, so I trekked on in my green plaid winter socks. A little farther down the road, I came upon a bubbling brook, with crystal clear spring water, lined by tall Birch trees filled with chirping songbirds. I quenched my thirst and pressed onward.

Ahead of me, nestled in a field of golden oats, I spied a pretty white horse. It lifted its head as I approached, nicked a soft greeting and trotted over to the edge of the field as I stumbled to a halt.

FYI: I'm not a fan of horses, and growing up on a farm with the temperamental steeds hadn't changed my mind one iota. They bite and kick and smell funny. And buck you off at the slightest inclination. No manners at all. I gave up the country life a long time ago for the creature comforts of the city, and I had no interest in reacquainting myself with farm animals. Even a heavenly pony with friendly, brown eyes.

The horse and I eyed one another. He lowered his head for me to pet, but I backed up a step and lifted my hands in self-defense. "Nothing personal, Mister Horse, but I'm in a hurry if you'll excuse me." I tried to step around him, but he blocked my way.

I put up hands of caution. "Stay back." I made a dismissive wave. "Go on, fly away like a good horse. Shoo, horse, shoo."

The damn horse actually smiled, then stamped a hoof as if he were trying to tell me something. It was then I noticed he was bridled and saddled for riding.

"Forget it, Mister Horse," I said as I backtracked several steps. "Thanks for the offer, but I don't need a ride. I can find my own way, thank you very much."

The horse wouldn't let me pass down the golden cobblestone road. Finally, in desperation, I swung a leg over his back and settled into the saddle. Once my heart rate slowed, I took the reins in hand as I'd once done as a child and pressed my legs against his sides. "Giddy-up."

The horse clamped the bridle bit into his mouth and shot into the air. I let out a scream and clung to the saddle horn as we sped through the countryside in the direction of the mountains. With a mighty stride, the horse galloped over the crags and cloud tops until the last valley came into view. There, in the midst, sat the Golden City like a king's crown on a green velvet pillow.

I screamed my indignation and tightened my hold as the horse dove downward toward the golden streets intersecting in many directions. Startled celestial citizens gaped up at me as the horse's hooves came down on the golden avenue in a hasty landing. His hooves clattered to a stop in front of a white-columned brick mansion. The sign on the fence read: *Supervisor of Foreign Affairs.*

I scrambled out of the saddle. As my feet touched

the cobblestones, the white horse trotted off in the opposite direction leaving the bridle and saddle, along with my snake boots, resting at my feet. Not confident I was in the right place, I glanced up and down the golden street for a better option. Seeing none, I left them there, unlatched the gate and went up the steps to the front door and rang the bell. The Southern rock music I'd heard earlier had dissipated over the mountains. Here, in the Golden City, the background noise mixed with the murmur of conversation and the harmony of laughter against the backdrop of angelic singing. Scarlett had mentioned the Hallelujah Choir in her threats. Must be them. Nice.

The door swung open and Saint Pete stood on the threshold. "Good gracious, what are you doing here?"

"That's what I'd like to know." I rubbed my sore backside and pushed past him without an invitation. "You're supposed to be on top of these things," I accused in a gruff voice. "I told you I needed one of those damn flaming swords."

He closed the door behind me. "Watch your language, young lady. You're on hallowed ground."

I glanced at the richly paneled walls and plush Turkish carpet under my stocking feet. A crystal chandelier hung overhead, casting soft light over the foyer. "This is a nice place, Pete. Do you suppose I could have a glass of iced sweet tea with a lemon wedge? And, I hate to ask, but can I have another change of clothes? It's hot up here, and I had to hitch a ride on a horse."

He led me into a quaint French country kitchen. "Have a seat, young lady while I prepare a cool beverage." He snapped his fingers, and the jeans and flannel shirt were replaced with a knee-length navy blue sheath with matching pumps and a string of pearls.

"Thank you, much better," I said, and sat down at the glass-topped table in the breakfast nook. My surroundings were comfy and luxurious I noted, while I waited for him to join me which wasn't long.

Saint Pete set a glass of amber liquid on the table in front of me. "Now, if you would please explain the circumstances which caused you to be here. I didn't authorize your release."

I sipped the tea. "Lilith ambushed me and shut off the ventilator."

He shook his head in dismay. "This wasn't supposed to happen. Where's your sidekick, Scarlett?"

"Getting her beauty sleep, I suppose. I took off on my own."

"Which is why you ended up in trouble."

I shrugged. "So send me back."

"Sorry, but you entered the Pearly Gates of your own accord, and there is nothing to be done. I'm not in the position to reverse your decision."

"Wrong," I corrected him. "I entered wrought iron gates. And I thought you were the Boss? Isn't your word law here?"

He frowned. "Those gates are supposed to be locked." He got up from the table and crossed the kitchen where a red telephone rested on the bar. He pressed a large silver button.

"How may I help you, Saint Peter?" a voice echoed from the speaker.

"Send a messenger to Dixieland Salon ASAP. I want Scarlett Cantrell back here. Pronto. And see if you can locate Sonya. She has some explaining to do. Death

Angel, indeed."

"Yes, sir. Dwayne is available for immediate dispatch, and Sonya is back at Hit Squad headquarters."

Saint Pete turned to gaze at me with kindness. "You have my profound apology, Jolene. This incident is entirely my fault. I should've realized you and Scarlett weren't equipped to take on Lilith. She's too powerful for human spirits. She requires my best warrior angels. I see that now. She was even able to pull the wool over Sonya's eyes. I believe it's time for her to retire. She's earned it, and there's a new guy that's perfect for the position." He smacked his hand against the marble-topped bar. "However, the bucks stops here, and because of my mistake, I will see that you're promoted to a bigger and better mansion in the best neighborhood in the northern quadrant of Paradise. After your trial, that is."

I squared my shoulders and gave him a determined smile. "I don't want a mansion in the sky. I want to go home to my red-brick house on Pinecone Lane."

"Impossible. I told you that."

"And you admitted you're responsible for my death," I reasoned. "The least you can do is give my life back."

"It would take an act of God to achieve such a request."

"Well, this is Heaven, isn't it? I assume *He's* here?"

His eyes bugged. "Young lady! One doesn't approach the throne with such a flippant attitude."

"Oh, I didn't mean me. This is your mistake to fix." I drank the tea and set the glass on the table. "It's the right thing to do. I'm sure you don't want a scandal like this to get out? What would the Headmaster say to that?"

He raised a brow. "Are you blackmailing me?"

"Of course not. I'm merely speculating. However, what would the Council of Noble Purposes say about your miscalculation?"

He made a snorting sound of disbelief. "You wouldn't dare approach the Council."

"Try me," I blustered, and then wondered if I shouldn't back off a mite. His face matched his thatch of red hair.

The doorbell sounded, breaking the building tension between us.

"Ah, they're here," he said in a calm voice. "Now we can get to the bottom of this and perhaps find a working solution for everyone involved."

"Which is getting me back home and Scarlett on to Scotland."

Scarlett, still dressed for Earth, came into the kitchen. Sonya trailed behind in her Mrs. Santa Claus duds. She stood awkwardly facing Saint Peter. Her merry eyes had lost their twinkle, and I felt kinda sorry for her. Poor ole gal.

Scarlett slid up next to me. "So this is where you disappeared to," she whispered. "Really, Jolene, you could've left a note."

Saint Pete placed a gentle hand on Sonya's sagging shoulders. "You're losing your delicate touch, my dear, and I'm afraid it's time for a change. I can't have my best Death Angel missing the mark. How about a long vacation on the planet of your choice? When you get back, the Council will have made a decision regarding your next assignment."

"I'm sorry, Boss. I don't know how I could've miscalculated my aim. I had the subject in my sights, and then poof, this brash, young woman screwed up the shot." She turned and gave me the evil eye. "These days young people don't know how to mind their own business. I swear the Earth is in need of another good flood. That would teach the upstarts to stay in their place."

I stuck my tongue out at her in response. Scarlett gave me a swift kick under the table, and I shot her a bird.

Saint Pete went on, "You're dismissed, for now, Sonya. Report to Personnel for additional instructions."

The former Death Angel gave me and Scarlett one last baleful glare, and then spun on her black patent leather pumps and disappeared out of the kitchen.

With Sonya's exit, he turned his attention on Scarlett. "Now that I've dealt with Sonya's flop, it's your turn. Once again, you broke the rules, and I'm sending you to the Peace Corps for a long, extended stint. If they can't whip you into shape, then you'll be referred to the Department of Transportation for your departure to Saturn. The rings are due for a cleaning, and you'll be perfect for the job."

She fluttered with dismay. "Please, Boss, you have no idea what I go through dealing with Jolene. She's stubborn and strong-willed."

"Oh, I think I have some idea of what you're experiencing, Scarlett," he said with a sigh of impatience. "Especially since you display the same attributes. You're a thorn in my side."

"I broke no rules," she began, and was silenced with a look.

I remained the silent observer. To be honest, the long, confusing trip was beginning to tell on me, and I stifled a yawn with the back of my hand. Weakness washed over me, and I felt a sudden anxiety I'd never experienced before in my physical life. Something was up. Something bad. My senses spun, and I laid my head down on the glass surface. I only listened with half an ear until Pete said, "I'll check the situation out for myself. Stay put. I'll be back in a flash."

I lifted my head to find Scarlett staring at me. "You beat everything, you know, Jolene? I should've kept my mouth shut about your momma being on the list. Next time, I'll just mind my own business!"

"There won't be a next time."

"Oh, yeah. I forgot. You're dead."

"I am—dead—aren't I?"

"Appears so."

"Does it take long to adjust?"

She waved a dismissive hand. "Not for most normal people like me." There was arrogant pride in her voice. "However, I suspect you might take a little longer. You're stranger than most."

"My family would agree with you." I swallowed back a sob. "Damn, Scarlett. My family. Lilith is out to seduce Roddy. Just before she pulled the plug, she bragged to me how she's going to destroy their marriage. I failed, Scarlett. I let down my family."

Scarlett drifted over to the table and sat in the chair across from me. "No, we failed. We're partners in this crazy situation, and I share the blame. Don't be too hard on yourself. And really, Heaven isn't so bad. Even without sex. The weather never changes, and you get to explore the universe on your time off. I particularly

149

love the Galaxy Mountains on horseback at this time of year."

I feigned a smile as my gaze swept the kitchen. "Where's Pete? Isn't he back yet?"

She let out a strained laugh. "It takes a little while to see if he can get your life back."

Chapter Fifteen
Dream Weaver

"I'm starved." I strode over to the pristine white cabinets and rummaged through them until I found a box of crackers. "I'm sure Pete won't mind if I have a small snack while waiting for him to return with the verdict." I set the box down on the butcher block counter, and opened the icebox and found a block of cheese and the pitcher of tea. I set them both on the counter next to the box of crackers and turned to Scarlett. "Join me?"

"Must you continue to refer to him as Pete?" Her tone reflected her displeasure. "His rank as Saint entitles him to a certain amount of respect. However, bein' dead ain't no excuse for bad manners."

I fixed a plate of crackers and cheese and sat down at the table across from her. "He's not complaining," I pointed out. "Besides, if I'm a royal pain in the ass, they'll be more likely to send me home."

She rolled her eyes. "I wouldn't count on it. You're here to stay, Claiborne."

Thankfully Saint Pete interrupted our lively discussion. My patience had all but taken a hike, and I wasn't in the mood for a boxing match with Scarlett. Every second away from home meant greater danger for Billie Jo and Roddy's marriage, and I was aching to join the living—although I hadn't figured out how to drive Lilith away.

"Well, I have news," he said without drama, and without a smile. "It cost me a promotion, but at least I'm not being demoted. Although, because of this debacle, there's another note of reprimand in my file."

"And?" I asked with bated breath, not at all interested in his latest putdown. "What's the verdict? Am I stuck here?"

He joined us at the table. The tension eased from his face, however, his eyes remained sharp and focused on me. "It took all I had to convince the Council to reverse its ruling, but you've been granted a reprieve. Scarlett, too."

A sigh of relief slipped out as I contemplated his words. I stood to my feet. "How do I get back?"

"Have a seat," he ordered. "There are a new set of rules. And I mean follow them this time." He directed a stern glance at Scarlett. "No wavering. The Council is adamant on this. Obey or pack your gear for Saturn. Got it?"

Her eyes blazed, but she inclined her head in compliance. "I'll do my best, but by now you realize how hard it is to keep her," she jerked her head toward me, "in line. I don't believe it's fair of the Council to hold me responsible for her actions."

"Never mind about that, Scarlett, just pay attention. Your future depends on you getting this right." Saint Pete pulled a crisp white sheet of parchment from his inside jacket pocket. "No interruptions while I outline the rules. I'll answer your questions afterward. Okay, here are the new and final set of rules you must abide by or face permanent banishment from Heaven. This comes all the way from the highest authority, so pay attention. This is a one-time dispensation never to be repeated henceforth." He rolled out the parchment. "Rule number one applies only to you, Jolene."

I leaned forward with an eager face and an open ear. No way was I going to screw up this last chance to save Billie Jo and Roddy's marriage. Sure, I wanted to return to the living, but mostly I wanted to save my youngest sister the pain and humiliation of a nasty divorce. Plus, there was another life at stake—her baby. Giving one's life was a small sacrifice to give him or her a happy, secure home life with two committed parents.

He continued, "You have been granted three short moments of physical manifestation into the corporeal dimension…"

I gasped with the impact and quickly clamped a hand over my mouth at his stern expression. Scarlett looked as if she'd swallowed a sour lemon drop.

"…to enlist help from your family members. However, because this action will require a great deal of life energy, the negative influence on your physical body will be substantial. In fact, it could destroy the remaining life energy you still have so think before you act."

Shocked, I blurted out, "How is that possible? I'm here."

"Technically, yes, you are," he replied. "However, as I just stated, this is a one-time event. It was arranged in the earthly dimension for the doctors to continue life-saving measures on your physical body long after they should've called your death. In human terms, you are now experiencing a near-death event. Your family is at this moment gathered together in the ICU waiting room for an update from the doctors. If I've answered your question, I'll continue with the rules. Time is short, and I need to get you both to the train station."

Thrilled with the news, I clamped my jaw shut and clasped my hands in my lap to still the excitement. Scarlett offered no comment, just stared at me with undisguised jealousy.

"Again, I caution you to use your physical manifestations wisely. Each event has consequences, and will only last for five minutes at the most. Five minutes, Jolene. Remember that fact. You can appear in solid human form for the equivalent of fifteen minutes. During your time in the corporeal world, you are bound by physics like any other human. If a human can't do it, neither can you." He lifted two fingers. "Rule number two. You may seek the help of a psychic or medium. I checked the books, and Madame Mia is on the list of approved spiritualists. If she's willing to listen and advise, go for it.

"Number three. Forget the Golden Rule. Do whatever it takes to extract Lilith from her chosen lair. There will be no accounting of wrongdoing. Show no mercy. Just get her gone. Number four. Use the swords of light wisely." Here he looked up from the parchment and eyed us both. "Yes, you will both be issued a temporary carry license. However, please be careful with them. Don't point it unless you intend to use it. They're powerful and unforgiving. You'll have a brief lesson by the archangel Hazell before departing for the station. Any questions?"

I lifted my hand. "How do you defeat a succubus?"

"Remember this, she's a dream weaver. You must catch her at her most vulnerable point, and that would be during her victim's dream state, and all her energy will be focused on seduction—therefore she'll be open to attack. But you must catch her unaware. That's key to defeat. Once she's in seduction mode, plant your swords of light between her shoulder blades. Time it perfectly, and Lilith will be vaporized."

"Why didn't you give us this information before?" I questioned point-blank, a little perturbed. "It would've saved me a lot of time and heartbreak."

His brow furrowed. "I don't make the rules. I just enforce them. Now if you two are ready, Hazell is waiting down on the green for your lesson." He withdrew two crisp white tickets from his inside jacket pocket and thrust them across the table at us. "Hurry, there's no time to delay." Faintly in the distance, a train whistle sounded. "Ah, the first warning. You have precisely ten bells before it pulls out of the station."

Saint Pete snapped his fingers, and once again I was clad in my former attire of jeans, flannel shirt, and boots. Good for demon hunting, but not for kick-ass warrior princesses with an ax to grind. "Come on, Saint Pete, can't you give us something that looks a bit more like warriors? You know to build up our courage."

In a blink of an eye, I found myself garbed in a pair leggings with really cool high-heeled boots that rode up past my knees. The warrior top I was currently wearing complimented the rest of the outfit. Scarlett on the other hand for some reason was modeling a two-piece outfit that looked a bit skimpy to me but would give her freedom to move.

Before I could thank Pete, we warrior princesses were transported to the green where we faced a giant blond with a long, flaming sword in hand. The angel cast us both a surprised look and said in a deep bass voice, "I can see I have my work cut out for me. Here." He thrust the flaming sword in my hand and produced another for Scarlett.

Surprised by the lightness of the weapon, I parried a few times for practice, then turned my attention to my angelic instructor.

"The first lesson of sword fighting," he began, "is to master the basics. It is important to know how to hold your sword. Don't wave it around, and never point it unless you're prepared to use it." A sword appeared in his hand. "Now I will demonstrate the proper way to hold the sword correctly and safely."

I mimicked his actions as did Scarlett. Next, he showed us the basic footwork of advance and retreat. Once we felt comfortable, he faced off with us. After a few rounds—turns out Scarlett's a natural—he nodded approval.

The train whistle blasted another warning. "Time's up," he said, sheathing his sword. "Remember to keep your swords sheathed and in the downwards position at all times until ready to use. Go with God."

In a blink that was almost as fast as Saint Pete's, we found ourselves at a quaint, yellow wooden train depot with brown trim and old benches positioned around the platform for easy use. The man at the window punched our tickets as the train rumbled into the station and coasted to a stop. White smoke belched from its tall stack.

"All aboard." The green-capped conductor swung down from the train and landed with a thunk on the wooden-planked platform. "All departing souls please have your tickets ready."

The conductor took our tickets and directed us to our seats in the front passenger car. Soon the cars were full of smiling commuters, and the locomotive whistled its imminent departure. I gazed in awe at our luxurious accommodations of green velvet seat cushions and mahogany paneling and trim.

We settled back against the cushions with a contented sigh as the train gained speed and passed through the Pearly Gates and down toward the Milky Way. Scarlett shifted her gaze from the window to me.

"I hope you have a plan." A ghost of a smile creased the corners of her ruby red lips. "I swear this whole incident has me turned inside out. Imagine," she twanged in an exaggerated Southern drawl. "My whole future hinges on my ability to swing a sword! I swear, Jolene, my social status has gone to hell since meeting you."

"Glad to oblige," I replied in my sweetest tone. "And yes, I do have a work-in-progress plan."

"And that would be?"

"Simple," I said in a confident tone. "First order of business is to establish communication. I'm going to burn one of my physical manifestation moments and enlist Deena's help. She may not like it, but she's going to be our point of contact among the living."

****

The first thing I noticed when we entered Earth's atmosphere was the silver thread attached to my side.

"It won't be long now," I told Scarlett. "I think we're close to the Georgia coastline. Isn't that Saint Simons Island down there?" I pointed to the small dot of land littered with condos and golf courses. "There's the old lighthouse."

Before she could answer, a booming voice announced, "All passengers for Whiskey Creek get ready to disembark on the next turn."

The train slowed and made a dip into the golden glow of sunrise. Soon it came to a screeching halt on a large, fluffy cloud on the outskirts of town, and Scarlett and I hopped off and watched it disappear over the horizon.

"Where to first?" Scarlett stifled a yawn behind her hand. "I could use a nap."

"No time for naps," I told her. "I want to swing by the hospital and check on my family. They've been through hell the past twenty-four hours, and I want to see them. And at the first chance I get, I'm going to arrange a little pow-wow with Deena."

"What if she won't cooperate? Deena's finicky about ghosts. She's not going to like us haunting Dixieland Salon."

"She'll get over it as soon as I can explain my situation. C'mon, we're running out of time."

Together, we zipped over the rooftops of homes and businesses until we reached Whiskey Creek General Hospital. In the room where my body lay connected to a zillion machines, my family had gathered, including my daughter, Becky.

Dr. Moore was saying, "We were able to resuscitate her. She's stable for now. However, we're cautious in our prognosis."

Daddy, who held Mama's hand in a tight grip, asked, "What happened to cause this setback, Dr. Moore?"

The young doctor smoothed his ruffled hair. "Well, to be honest, we believe someone, either accidentally, or on purpose, turned off the ventilator."

Boy, talk about dropping a bomb! Evidently, the doctor wasn't from the South. The domino effect was explosive as my family went nuts with shock, anger, and fear. Scarlett and I watched the raw emotions from the ceiling as their raised voices permeated the quiet ICU. Heads swung from all directions at the disturbance.

"Son-of-a-bitch," Daddy roared. His eyes bugged, and his face reddened. "What's goin' on around here?"

Dr. Moore grabbed his arm in a strong grip. "Calm down, Mr. Tucker. We've notified the police. They're interviewing the night staff now. However, I need you and your family to remain calm. There are other patients in this critical care unit."

Daddy shook off the doctor's grip. "Don't tell me to remain calm when someone tried to kill my daughter twice," he said in a lowered steely tone.

"We don't know the facts yet—"

"Yet, the police are here investigating a possible attempted murder," Mama cut the doctor off.

"Attempted murder?" Deena shot Ryder a panicked look. "Good gracious, who would commit such a vicious crime?"

Ryder took her hand. "I believe we should take this outside to the waiting room. I'd like to place a call to Chief Nichols. He owes me a favor, and this seems like the time to collect on that debt."

Becky clutched her stomach. "I think I'm going to be sick."

Billie Jo clamped a hand over her mouth and tore out of Roddy's grasp. "Oh, God, me too." She held out her hand toward Becky. "There's a ladies room just outside the unit." Hand in hand, they exited the room.

"I'd better keep an eye on them," Roddy said with a worried expression. "All this drama isn't good for the baby, and Billie Jo refuses to go home. God, she's so stubborn."

"Like Jolene," Deena added with a sob. "I believe I'll join them in the waiting room."

"Ryder is right." Mama tugged on Daddy's hand. "Let's go make some calls. I have a connection of my own."

Subdued, the rest of the family trailed behind Roddy out of the intensive care unit and to the waiting room. Scarlett and I waited as Dr. Moore completed his examination on my listless body, and leaving a nurse behind, left the same way as my family.

"That was an interesting conversation," Scarlett said in an off-handed manner. "Attempted murder. Too bad we can't rat out Lilith. She'd disappear in a heartbeat if the cops were hot on her trail."

"Damn, Scarlett, you're right," I pointed out. "The person known as Lilith Lacewell wouldn't take the chance of going to jail. But how to prove it? There's no evidence. And even if the police dusted for prints on the ventilator, how could they determine Lilith's fingerprints with so many medical personnel having touched the switch?"

She touched the sheathed sword at her side. "Personally, I hope we get to stab her in the back when she's doing her seduction dance with Roddy. It's been awhile since I've stuck it to someone, and I'd just as rather it be her. Slimy bitch."

My eyes strayed to the nurse straightening the sheets over me. "I'd prefer we set the police on her. I'm not fond of the idea of her seducing Billie Jo's husband while he's sleeping. C'mon, let's see if I can get Deena's attention. The sooner I make contact, the sooner she can point the finger of suspicion at Lilith Lacewell."

Deena wasn't in the waiting room, but we arrived in time to hear Mama drop another bombshell.

"Well, he's on his way." She snapped shut her cell phone and dropped it into her purse. "Sam is catching the next flight out of Jackson Hole, Wyoming. He'll get a shuttle flight from Atlanta and rent a car in Albany. He should arrive late tonight. I told him he could stay with us at the farm, Harland."

Daddy nodded his head in approval. "Good man, Sam Bradford. It's a relief to know he's on his way. He'll get to the bottom of this. Yes, siree, Sam's a good man to have around in a pinch."

My spirit soared with the announcement, and I zipped through the roof and into the endless blue skies above doing flips and swirls through fluffy white cumulus clouds.

Hot damn, Bradford was returning to Whiskey Creek!

Chapter Sixteen
Come Fly with Me

Scarlett and I returned to Dixieland Salon to find Deena frantically cleaning an already spotless shop. Scarlett discreetly retired to the facial room for a quick nap, leaving me alone with my sister. Now that the time to materialize had arrived, I found myself nervous and uncertain how to proceed. One doesn't just magically appear out of thin air. The surprise of seeing me here in the shop instead of the ICU could very well send her into shock or a nervous breakdown. Deena had been restless and agitated for weeks leading up to her wedding, and my diving into near death had only exasperated her condition.

Caution was the keyword here.

My opportunity came when she'd worn herself down to a frazzle and had plopped down in an exhausted heap on her office sofa. I drifted through the doorframe and watched her for several minutes. Her eyes were closed, and her breathing even, if just a mite jerky, and I could detect the soft sniffle of tears.

Saint Pete said I could materialize into solid form for five minutes. Still, I remained invisible, uncertain of her reaction. The silence of the salon was complete. Even the hum of the refrigerator was absent here in the front office. With slow deliberation, I wafted into the room until I stood before the plush sofa. I whispered the quick prayer he'd given me and willed myself present.

"Deena, honey, open your eyes."

Her eyes popped open, and with a screech of delight, she launched herself at me. I caught her body against mine, and we both staggered to the hardwood floor. We rolled over laughing as we'd done as children. She pushed a tangle of bangs from her eyes and cried, "Oh, Jolene, you startled me. Shame…"

Her voice trailed off as her gaze swept my warrior attire. "What are you doing here in that getup?" She climbed shakily to her feet. "Wait a minute. I was just at the hospital not less than two hours ago. You were in a coma." She looked wildly about. "How can you be here with no aftereffects?" She stepped back from my outstretched hand, a hand pressed to her lips. "You can't be here. I'm hallucinating. No, I'm dreaming, caught in a nightmare."

A pang of remorse ripped through me, knowing I'd made a huge miscalculation with my sister. Deena was still too fragile to accept my physical presence, but now I had no choice but to move ahead quickly and bring control and reason to my sudden appearance.

"You're not dreaming," I said in an even tone meant to calm her. "I'm real. You can touch me and see I'm real."

She struggled for breath and looked as if she might faint. "No, don't touch me. Stay away, or I'll scream."

"Okay, enough time wasted. I have five minutes before I disappear and you're going to listen to me. Got it?" I bolted toward her and grabbed her by the arm, and keeping a tight grip shoved her into one of the chairs facing her desk. "Allow me to refresh your memory." I pinched her hard on the upper arm. "Bring back memories?"

"Ouch!" She jerked her arm out of my grasp. "Knock it off, Jolene. I swear to God, you get on my last nerve."

I gave her my best sisterly smile. "As you do mine, *Sister Dearest*, but that's beside the point. Now, do you believe me?"

A bewildered look crinkled her face. "I'm divided on this one, Jolene, but I'm willing to meet you halfway. You've pulled some stupid stunts in the past two years, but this one takes the cake. How is this possible?"

"I don't have time for a lengthy explanation, but I'm here because of a monumental mistake on Heaven's part. Scarlett and I are here to right a wrong."

She groaned. "Scarlett's here? Why am I not surprised?"

I pointed to my wristwatch. "I have three remaining minutes left, so listen up." She nodded, and I continued, "Bradford is on his way here. Lilith is the one who turned off the ventilator in an attempt to stop me. He needs to find enough evidence to convince the police to investigate her. She's not who she presents herself to be, Deena. She's a demon from the pit of Hell."

Doubt came into her eyes. "You want me to convince Sam that Lilith Lacewell is a demon? Good gracious, Jolene. Sam Bradford will never go for it. He doesn't believe in the afterlife. This is crazy. You're crazy. It won't work."

I blew out a frustrated breath as the precious seconds ticked away. "Yes, it will and don't underestimate Bradford's belief system. I don't have time to explain but leave ghosts and demons out of it, sis. Just point the finger of suspicion at Lilith. Give him a reason to investigate her. If she comes under the police microscope, she'll be forced to disappear."

"This is so confusing. I don't know what to do."

"Go with your gut, sis," I encouraged. "Have I ever steered you wrong?"

Her brows spiked. "Oh, yeah, many times."

"She's after Roddy."

That got her attention. "How do you know?"

"She told me just before she pulled the plug."

"What does she want with Roddy? He's happily married."

"Simple. She wants sex. Lilith is a succubus, Deena. She's after his life energy through his semen."

"OMG! I've never heard of such a thing. A succubus? Really? You're for real?"

"Yes, Deena. I'm not trying to shovel manure at you. I'm trying to save Billie Jo's marriage. Keep an open mind, please."

She twisted her lip between her teeth. "I'll try, Jolene, but you're right, this could destroy Billie Jo if she caught him cheating. Even possibly cause her to miscarry the baby."

"The Devil's mistress doesn't care about life. I'm proof of that."

"Okay, I'm in. What do I do first?"

"First thing is to keep Lilith out of my hospital room. Ryder has the chief's ear. See if he can request Diamond Pressley as my bodyguard. She's trustworthy and loyal and on the police force. This will give the family a break from the constant vigil. Bradford is scheduled to arrive late tonight. See if you can arrange

165

to meet him out at the farm and speak with him in private. I don't want Mama or Daddy to be involved in any way. Hopefully, Bradford will take it from there. I know he's no longer on the force, but that won't stop him. Just point him in the right direction and let him run."

"What about Roddy and Billie Jo? How do I keep Lilith away from him when he's renovating her shop?"

"Don't worry about that. Lilith works her magic during the darkest hours of night, and that's where Scarlett and I come in. We'll be on guard duty tonight. If she gets anywhere near him, we'll slash her to pieces with our swords."

"I was wondering about that sword. I know I shouldn't ask, but how do you get yourself in these situations?"

"Because I'm a neurotic, control freak and can't mind my own business. However, I've learned my lesson this time around, I promise." I raised my right hand. "I pledge to turn a blind eye to any and all ghosts, murders, and mysteries if I make it out of this alive. I promise."

She didn't challenge my statement but asked instead, "What about the shop? Should I shut it down?"

"No, business as usual. We can't afford to lose our health insurance. Hire a manager and a couple of additional stylists if the staff can't handle the workload, but keep the doors open by all means."

Her smile didn't quite reach her eyes. "I don't know how I'm going to explain all this to Ryder. We haven't had much time together since our wedding. And on top of everything else he has the added worry of his parents. They have to somehow get back to

Atlanta for Helen's next chemo treatment. We were going to drop them off before we caught our flight to Hawaii. I guess he'll have to make a quick trip to Atlanta tomorrow."

Guilt assaulted me at her expression of mute wretchedness. Geez, I'd been so consumed with my own problems that I hadn't spent one millisecond considering Deena. She and Ryder should be, right now this moment, off on an exciting honeymoon. Instead, they were trapped here in Whiskey Creek by unforeseen circumstances.

I took her hands in mine. "Sis, I'm so sorry I spoiled your reception and honeymoon, but I promise to make it up to you both when this is over. Which won't be long if my plan works out. Please, hang in there and know that all your dreams will come true in the long run."

She squeezed my hand. "They already have, Jolene. You're here now, and I'm Mrs. Ryder Matheson."

A feeling of weightlessness spread through me, and I knew only seconds remained before I would rejoin the dead. "My time is up. Please do as I asked, and if you need me, leave a note in the facial room. Scarlett and I are using it as our mission control."

"You're haunting the salon?" Her laughter rang loudly. "I never imagined those words would be music to my ears."

With her amusement assaulting my ears, I drifted out of the office and back to the facial room for a little shut-eye. Tonight, Scarlett and I would stand guard over Billie Jo and Roddy's house for any intruders of the nasty kind. Seeing Scarlett curled up on the loveseat, I settled into the rocking chair and fell into a dead sleep if you know what I mean.

****

Nightfall comes early this time of the year, and twilight had turned to darkness when Scarlett and I shot through the ceiling of the salon and soared high above the rooftops of buildings and homes in the center of town. The workday was over, stores were locking up, and supper was on the stove in most of the homes. We circled the statue in the courthouse square, upsetting a nest of sparrows in the tall, ancient evergreen magnolia, and skimmed down Main Street until we reached Park and Sixth Street and the beautiful old historic clapboard house Billie Jo and Roddy were painstakingly restoring back to its 1890s glory.

Over a century old, the two-story house still needed a ton of work and lots of paint, but I knew Billie Jo loved the place. Roddy had hated it upon first sight, but my sister chiseled him down until he caved. They'd bought it at an auction for a fraction of its worth, and on weekends and holidays, both worked tirelessly to put the grand ole dame back together again.

I liked the pale pink wooden house with crisp white trim and spacious front porch. A fall wreath of red and orange leaves graced the glass-paneled decorative front door. Warm, yellow light spilled from the windows and from my perch in the crape myrtle tree, all three vehicles were parked in the driveway.

Perfect, they were all safe at home.

"We're not alone," Scarlett said from the branch above me. "Lilith's henchmen have arrived." She pointed to several black shapes and glowing eyes lurking in the neighboring yards, then patted the sword strapped to her back. "I hope we get to use these bad boys. I'm aching for a fight."

"Any sign of Lilith?" I forced myself to remain calm and focused. My gaze swept the roof of the house for any movement or shadows. "And don't be too quick to start a fight. We'd lose, you know. We're outnumbered and amateurs."

Scarlett joined me on my branch. "Speak for yourself. I happened to be pretty good with this thing. As for Lilith, I don't believe she's arrived for the party."

"Stay here and keep a lookout," I directed. "I'm going to scope out the inside for any sign of trouble. Lilith could be anywhere."

She tapped her sheathed sword. "Are you sure I can't rout a few nasty imps out of hiding? I'm bored."

"Keep your panties on, Scarlett. I'll be back in a jiffy."

The cloudy night sky kept the moon under wraps, and I skirted around the front porch to the backyard where a dim light shone above the steps to the screened porch. I moved ahead eagerly and passed through the rear door and into the brightly lit kitchen. Solemn voices drifted back from the dining room, and I could tell by the conversation they were discussing the doctor's latest prognosis on my deteriorating condition.

I wafted through the doorway for a quick peek at my sister and her family. Roddy was at the head of the table, and Lynette sat to his left. Billie Jo, picking at her meatloaf with her fork, occupied the chair to his right. Her weary face looked pinched and sad and frighteningly pale. Although I wanted to linger, I needed to check out the rest of the rambling house. The downstairs contained no surprises from the spirit world. I drifted upstairs to the master bedroom. Nothing. Lynette's room, clean as a whistle. The nursery, empty. Not much work had been done in here, only Lynette's old crib had been set up by the window. Evidently, a theme had yet to be chosen. I paused there over the light oak crib and imagined the new life that would soon occupy this space. A nephew if Lilith was correct, a little boy to complete their family.

I finished my sweep of the house and found nothing of concern. Downstairs, I paused in the kitchen as Billie Jo and Lynette cleaned the dinner dishes. From the living room, a TV blasted. Since he was Lilith's primary target, I would verify Roddy's safety, then rejoin Scarlett outside. Roddy, stretched out on his recliner, was flipping channels when I wafted in from the kitchen. He yawned several times, and I knew it wouldn't be too long before went upstairs to bed. Roddy retired early, according to Billie Jo.

Not finding any paranormal threat in the house, I surmised Lilith was nowhere in the vicinity, and I could rejoin Scarlett. We would continue to monitor the house from the safety of the trees and intercede if Lilith appeared. Which I suspected would occur in the wee hours of the morning. Good thing, Scarlett and I had caught a few extra winks.

Outside the moon hung low in the crisp night sky, and a gentle breeze rattled autumn leaves from a big sweet gum tree and tall pine in the backyard. Scarlett was still hunkered down in the skinny crape myrtle tree.

"Several more of Lilith's cronies arrived while you were gone," she said when I settled down beside her on the branch. "No hideous warriors of hell. Just pesky imps with no leadership. We could take them, you know. Wipe 'em out in one sweep."

"Too risky," I muttered. "And it would blow our cover and ruin any chance of an ambush."

"I'm fairly certain they know we're here."

"What did you do?"

"Not a cotton-pickin' thing, dumbass," she snickered. "I've been ghosting for a while now. I'm good at what I do. You, however, have no concept of stealth."

"Are you saying it's my fault?"

Scarlett's eyebrows shot up, but instead of answering, she unsheathed her sword of lightning, and screamed, "Fight like hell, because here they come!"

Chapter Seventeen
Chances Are

I snapped out of my paralysis at the sight of two, bulb-eyed *things* barreling toward me, their dark wings whirring and strings of yellow sulfurous ribbons pouring from their open, snarling mouths. Profanity filled the cool autumn night with spews of hatred and damnation for the heavenly as one of the beasts clashed with Scarlett in midair.

"Holy crap," I screamed in a blind panic and drew my sword and scrambled off the branch to meet the incoming missile speeding toward me. With both hands clasped on the hilt of the sword, I could hardly maintain flight, so I dipped close to the ground and did a backflip as the bat-like *thing* took a swing at me with his fiery sword. It grazed my ankle, and a burning sting set my flesh on fire. Wounded, I hit the ground and rolled over on my back. Our swords met and clashed. Sparks flew in every direction as we fought for dominance.

"Get on your feet!" I heard Scarlett yell somewhere above me. "He has the advantage."

Screaming with fear and frustration, I tried to recall the basics of sword fighting taught by the archangel Hazell, but my mind grew hazy as the enemy's sword pricked my upper arm. Pain blazed through me, and I barely parried the next jab. From my position on the ground, I watched his fiery sword arch upwards, and I knew I was done for. I closed my eyes and said a quick prayer.

"Jolene, honey, open your eyes."

My eyes popped open with surprise and joy at Granny Tucker's voice, and the sweet scent of Grandpa's pipe tobacco. With renewed determination and vigor, I met the imp's attack with a fiery slash. The blow sent him spinning back through the air, giving me time to stagger to my feet and waft up to the first branch on a leafy holly tree. Through the prickly leaves, I watched with awe and admiration as Scarlett slashed a wide, blistering path through a legion of imps. Screams and cries filled the air as she slashed through dark wings and scattered the enemy. An eerie shriek seemed to hang in the thick night air before they retreated beyond the edge of trees bordering Sixth Avenue.

The back porch light flicked on, the screen door opened and Billie Jo and Roddy stepped out. "I'm telling you, Roddy, I heard a commotion out here. Get your flashlight and see if the neighbor's tomcat is on the prowl again. I definitely heard a scream."

"Damn cat," Roddy growled. "I think it's time we get a dog. That'll put an end to his nightly invasions."

From my perch behind a screen of leaves, I watched Roddy go back into the house, leaving Billie Jo silhouetted in the pool of light. She held onto the porch rail and gazed out into the backyard. Her cap of blonde hair shimmered under the bright light, and I could almost feel the tension and sadness emanating from her when she touched her stomach and sighed.

Scarlett joined me on the branch. "They've gone for now, but they'll be back with reinforcements. Are you okay?"

I tried to move my stiff arm. "Not really. But I'll live," I added with a laugh. "However, you were magnificent. You make one hell of a warrior. I'm surprised Heaven hasn't made better use of your talents."

She sheathed her sword. "Thanks, Claiborne. I wish I could say the same for you. Pitiful. Just pitiful."

I was too humiliated to be insulted. "I prefer pistols to swords."

The screen door opened and closed with a bang, and a flashlight beam swept the yard. "I don't see anything," Roddy's voice rang out.

"Check along the fence and in the trees," Billie Jo directed. "He likes the holly tree. God, only knows why. The leaves are stiff and prickly. Stupid cat."

The beam of light brushed the branches of the tall evergreen. "Nothing in the trees or along the fence, sweetie." The beam snapped off. "Whatever you heard is gone now. C'mon, let's go to bed. I'm bushed."

"You go on without me," Billie Jo said. "I'm going to call Becky for an update. She's staying the night at the hospital."

"Becky will call if there's any change, honey. We've been there most of the day. You need your rest. The baby…"

"I know what you're going to say, Roddy," Billie Jo's voice echoed with sarcasm. "I've heard it a thousand times from you and everyone else. Give it a rest, won't you?"

The screen door banged shut on his answer.

"What now?" Scarlett arched her back and stretched her arms high above her head. The top she wore outlined her enormous store-bought boobs.

I looked away and massaged my stiff arm. "We wait for Lilith. I have a feeling it's not gonna be long."

"Are you up for another fight with that arm and ankle injury?"

"Would you like to do this on your own?"

"Not hardly."

"Well, then, I'm all you've got. Any suggestions?"

"Only one."

"And that is?"

"Start praying because we haven't a snowball's chance in Hell of beating the enemy."

"Do you think Heaven will hear us?"

"I don't know, but it doesn't hurt to try."

I bowed my head and sent a heartfelt prayer heavenward. When I lifted my head, it was to find Scarlett's curious gaze glued on me.

"Well?" she asked. "Get any answers?"

"Only one."

"Care to share with your BFF?"

"Yeah. Fight like hell because here she comes!" I had barely gotten the words out of my mouth when, from across the street, a bank of thunderclouds rolled in with a rising gale that whipped the tops of the trees. The streetlights flickered, then went out, plunging the neighborhood into darkness.

All hell broke loose with one mighty roar in the form of a flash of lightning, and the boom of thunder. Freaked out, I toppled from the branch and landed on the ground with my sword still in its sheath. From above I heard Scarlett flutter crazily into the air and her scream of fury at being taken by surprise. Moments later, she fell from the sky and lay crushed and bent beside me.

I looked up at a hellish sight. The air was filled with roaring, fluttering wings as Lilith and her demon gang swirled around us, imprisoning us in their tight circle. In only moments, we were caught. They began to cheer and boast, their talons clicking their applause.

The streetlights came on. Lilith lifted my chin with her sharp talon, so I was staring into her red, gleaming, lust-filled eyes. "So you still want to fuck with me? Give up, Jolene. You can't defeat me." She cast her glance to the light shining in one of the upstairs windows. "Soon, he will be mine, and there will be no one to stop me."

The hoard of demons crackled with glee, their green eyes burning with fire, and I swung my gaze from them to the master bedroom window, and I knew as soon as the light was extinguished, Lilith would strike.

****

The night grew colder with each passing second in the enemy's clutches. Scarlett had finally roused and now sat compressed between two massive demon warriors. Her face reflected my bitterness and despair. Our swords had been confiscated and were propped against the trunk of a holly tree—approximately ten feet between us and a dozen triumphant imps just waiting for their turn to harass us.

For all intents and purposes, we were finished—defeated—with no hope of rescue. My prayer for help from above remained unanswered. Even the moon had retreated behind a thick, broiling thundercloud, turning the night sky slightly green. All eyes were fastened on Lilith, who in turn, had her lusty gaze fixed on the upstairs window.

Five minutes passed in slow agony while my brain

searched for a way out of our predicament. My thoughts jumbled. Nothing came to mind. Roddy's silhouette crossed the window. Lilith tensed, her beastly face grew tight and smug as her mouth stretched into a fang-bearing grin. The demons poked one another in fiendish delight as their leader drooled with anticipation.

The window plunged into darkness as the light extinguished. A mutter ran through the ranks, then Lilith shot into the night sky and dropped onto the roof and disappeared from sight. The demon gang went wild with celebration. Laughing with sinful drunkenness, they rolled and punched one another, each punch sending the group further into a mad frenzy. Wisps of rancid yellow breath blew out in hisses and grunts and profanity through jagged fangs.

Scarlett and I exchanged knowing looks but kept silent. I motioned my head toward our swords leaning against the holly tree. She nodded, and together we launched ourselves away from the group of tangled demons and scooped up our swords. With a twisted flop, I dove upward and immediately crashed to the ground and rolled into the tin garbage cans beside the garage. The sound exploded into the silent night. Dogs began barking and howling at the sudden noise.

Scarlett spun around and dove into the swirling mass of demons with her sword blazing. Screams and cries erupted as the demons fled her fiery blade. The group scattered and retreated as before. Atop the clanging garbage cans, I watched Billie Jo rush out the screen door and onto the back porch. Seeing my chance, I fluttered back into hiding.

"What the hell is going on out here?" she yelled into the darkness. "Roddy! Roddy! Get your ass down here with your gun. That damn tomcat is back."

Upstairs, the master bedroom light switched on to display Roddy's silhouette in the lighted window. From the roof came a blast of black light, its dark wings whirring as it shot upward and over the tree line.

"Well, that takes care of Lilith for the night," Scarlett boasted as she settled down beside me on the branch of the holly tree. "That was a brilliant plan, Jolene. Diving into those garbage cans and waking the neighborhood dogs." She chuckled. "Roddy won't be dreaming any time soon. Boy, Billie Jo's worked up."

"I didn't do it on purpose," I admitted with a lopsided smile. "I'm a ghostly klutz, and my shoulder is out of whack. I could use a massage."

She sheathed her sword. "Can't help you with that, but what do you say we head back to headquarters? I've earned a little R&R."

"Agreed. Let's leave before Billie Jo gets her gun and starts shooting at imaginary cats."

Exhausted but exhilarated by our victory, Scarlett and I left Billie Jo and Roddy searching the backyard for the tomcat and flew back to Dixieland Salon where a note from Deena took up space on the facial room counter. Sam Bradford was back in Whiskey Creek, and they both were headed for the hospital.

****

With my heart lodged firmly in my throat, I sank down through the hospital ceiling in my astral form and spied Deena hunched over the back of a chair in a troubled slumber, and my daughter Becky stretched out on the sofa with her eyes closed. I knew she wasn't sleeping by her restless movements. I allowed my gaze to stay with her for several more seconds before I shifted my attention to the tall, handsome man pacing the ICU waiting room like a caged tiger in a zoo.

Samuel Bradford. Here at last. I felt dizzy with relief and approached cautiously. I doubted he could pick up on my spiritual presence, and I suspected his ability to detect spirits had vanished the instant Vanessa van Allen, and Careen Halsey's double homicide case had been solved. (One of my misadventures better told elsewhere.)

No, he hadn't changed, but I had. After this latest mishap, I now saw the error of my ways and was ready to embrace a more sedate lifestyle. Learn to smell the roses along the way. To let go of everyone and everything. To let life unfold and live fearlessly.

Like Scarlett. She was so much more than I ever imagined. A true heroine fashioned for a rousing romantic tale. Flawed, yet courageous. Beautiful and faithful. She'd risked her position in Heaven to come to my aid. Her death marked the beginning of our friendship, and I now counted her as my best friend.

Deena moaned and lifted her head. "What time is it?"

"After midnight," Bradford replied in his husky voice. "When do you suppose they'll let me in to see Jolene? I'm tired of waiting."

Deena rose to her feet to arch her back. "I'm not sure, Sam, but it shouldn't be much longer. The nurse said they were changing a defective IV machine."

Becky rolled over and opened her eyes and sat up. "I'm going down to the cafeteria for coffee and give call Jacob a quick call and check on Hannah. Can I bring you guys a cup of coffee?"

"None for me, Becky," Deena said.

"Thanks, but no," Bradford echoed the same.

"I'll be back in fifteen minutes or so, Aunt Deena." Becky grabbed her purse and left the waiting room.

"I'm glad she's gone," Bradford said to Deena as soon as Becky disappeared down the hall. "I didn't want to discuss this in front of her, but after I visit with Jolene, I'm driving over to the police station. I want to speak with the detectives on the case, and see what they have to say about the hospital security videos. First thing, tomorrow morning, I'm going to pay Lilith Lacewell a visit and get a few answers. You're sure about her threats to Jolene?"

"I'm sure, Sam. There was something bad going on between those two. Jolene told us that Lilith wasn't who she presented herself to be."

"Anything else?"

Deena shifted uncomfortably, and I could see doubt enter her eyes, so I drifted over to her side and pinched her upper arm to alert her to my presence. She jumped at my touch, gave a yelp, and then gushed, "Yes. Jolene suspected Lilith was out for Roddy." She slowly surveyed the waiting room.

I gave her another pinch. Airhead. That's not enough motive for attempted murder.

Bradford reacted as I suspected he would. "That's not enough motive for attempted murder, Deena. The police will need more to bring her in for questioning. Let's hope there's some evidence on the security tapes of her being in the hospital at the time of the incident."

A nurse entered the waiting room. "Mr. Bradford, you may come in now. But only for a few minutes." Bradford grabbed up his hat from the chair and followed her down the hall to the double doors.

Although I wanted to speak with Deena, I knew this wasn't the time or place, and besides, I wanted to be present when he visited me. I twisted the silver thread around my finger as I trailed behind him to my glass-enclosed unit. The nurse left him at the door, and he went inside and up to my bed which was surrounded by beeping machines. He set his Stetson on the bed and clasped my hand in his.

"Hey, Claiborne, it's me, Sam." His deep, resilient voice broke. "You sure know how to get a fella's attention." He dashed a tear from his cheek. "C'mon, now, girl. Open those magnificent brown eyes and tell this ole cowboy you're ready to get up from this bed and hitch a ride out West. C'mon, Jolene, I know you can hear me. Give me a sign. Squeeze my hand, or better yet, open your eyes."

I drifted to his side and said in my loudest voice, "I'm here, Sam. Right here. At your side. Listen with your heart." I laid my hand on the hand over mine on the bed. "I hear you. I hear you."

He paused for a fraction of a second, and looked over his shoulder at the empty room, and then back down at my still body. "Jolene, listen to me, sweetie. I want you to fight with all the tenacity and stubbornness I've grown to love about you. I never should've left here without you, I know that now, and I regret not paying more attention to your reason for staying, for not giving you more time to work out your family's problems. I admire your unending love and devotion to them, and I shouldn't have been so hard with you. Perhaps if I'd stayed through Deena's wedding, I could've stopped this tragedy."

Seeing his distress, I willed my hand to move, but

again, my body refused to respond to my commands. Desperate to show some sign of life, I willed myself back into my body. A jolt of electricity shot through me as spirit and body reconnected. Major mistake. Unbearable pain ripped through me as I fully inhabited my physical form, and I instinctively knew I had only a second or two before my spirit would flee the burning agony.

The machines attached to my physical form let out several beeps, and I concentrated all of my willpower and energy to the hand clasped in Bradford's. It wasn't much, but it flinched a tiny fraction.

Feeling the movement, Bradford grasped my hand just as my spirit slipped free of its physical confines. "I knew you could hear me, Claiborne." He lifted my hand to his lips. "That's my girl. C'mon, do it again. Let's prove these doctors wrong."

I watched for five further minutes as he tried to coax another response from my lifeless body kept alive by the various connected machines and IV's. Finally, he seemed to give up and placed my limp hand back on the covers.

"You listen up, Claiborne. I've got to go to work and find the person or persons responsible for your being here, but I'll be back real soon." His voice rang with certainty. "You hang in there, sweetie, and keep fighting the good fight, and let me take care of the rest."

He placed a lingering kiss on my lips, grabbed his Stetson from the bed and settled it on his head, and with one last determined glance, he strode from the room.

Chapter Eighteen
Rock Around The Clock

The Whiskey Creek police station was housed in a squat, two-story red brick building near the historic district and downtown. I'd hitched a ride on the back bumper of Bradford's rented sedan from the hospital, and as we pulled into the deserted front parking, I noticed Chief Nichols police cruiser parked in his spot.

Bradford killed the engine and swung out of the driver's door. I followed in his wake up the stairs and through the front glass door to the front desk where a young male officer looked up and smiled at his approach. Officer Ralph Middleton, his badge read.

"Why if it isn't Detective Sam Bradford," he said, rising to his feet. "I didn't expect to see you again for a long time. What brings you back to these neck of the woods so soon?"

The two men shook hands. Bradford produced his badge. "It's Police Chief Bradford, now, and I'm here about the Claiborne case. It's rather important, and I'd like to have a word with the Chief if he's in."

"He's here, all right. Sometimes I wonder if the man ever goes home. Give me a minute, and I'll see if he's awake."

The officer disappeared down the hall. Several minutes passed before he returned and gave Bradford the go-ahead.

"He's as ornery as a grizzly bear in mating season, Sam, so watch out. You picked a mighty bad time for a visit. He's still sore at your leavin'. Said so, too. Added a few choice words that made my ears turn red. Maybe you might want to come back after he's had a long nap and a substantial breakfast."

"Sorry, Ralph, no time for naps and breakfast. I need answers. Good seeing you again." Bradford tipped his hat and strode down the hall to the chief's office. He rapped on the door and received a prompt answer.

"Come in," came a gruff voice.

I wafted in behind Bradford as he pushed through the door and into the office. I noticed the chief's face, and bloodshot eyes looked dog tired and put off. Chief Nichols indicated the chair facing his desk. I perched on the edge of the desk facing both men.

"You have no jurisdiction here," he growled. "However, I know you and the Claiborne woman had a thing before you left town so I guess I can allow you a little leeway. But don't get in my way, Bradford. This is a simple case of clumsy fingers pushing the wrong button."

Bradford's eyes narrowed. "Did you just say it was a case of hospital negligence? If so, I'm sure the family would be mighty interested in your assessment. I've seen lawsuits filed for less."

"I said no such thing, Bradford. Don't put words in my mouth or I'll kick your sorry ass out of here. I warn you, this is an ongoing investigation, and I'll brook no interference from you."

"You're right. I don't have jurisdiction, but I know plenty of people who do, Chief." Bradford took off his Stetson and held it in both hands, his eyes never leaving

Nichols' stern face. "I'm not leaving here until I'm satisfied there's no foul play involved. I can make myself a pain in your ass. I've done it before, and I'll do it again if it produces results."

"That shiny new police chief's badge has gone to your head, Bradford. I'd be careful of what I say if I were you."

Bradford leaned forward. "I didn't come here to box words with you, Chief. I'm here because someone I care deeply for was severely injured in a drive-by shooting on the day of her sister's wedding. Add in the suspicious incident at the hospital, and you can see why I'm concerned for her safety. As a matter of fact, I would appreciate it if you placed an officer in her room as a safeguard. Someone like Diamond Pressley. She's familiar with Jolene and her family, and capable of deterring any further *accidents*."

Chief Nichols stretched backward and put his hands behind his head. "What do you know that I don't?"

Bradford dodged the question. "I'm interested in seeing the hospital security footage."

"Anyone, in particular, you're looking for?"

"Yeah, someone of interest."

"And who would that be?" His mouth twisted into a sardonic grin.

"Lilith Lacewell."

His grin vanished, and his brows drew down in thought. "Seems I've heard that name before. On a recent incident report. Hmmm, and I believe it involved the Claiborne woman's place of business." He sat up and leaned forward over his desk. "Let me check the computer files." The computer keyboard clicked several times. "Ah, yes, here it is. Officers Rivers and Ballard responded to a call last Friday morning at the salon. The report states that a heavy speaker fell from a top-shelf narrowly missing an employee's head."

"That employee was Jolene's mother, Annie Mae Tucker."

Chief Nichols shifted his gaze from the computer screen to Bradford. "And according to the report, Lilith Lacewell is the one who pushed Mrs. Tucker out of the way, thereby saving the woman's life." He sat back. "Now tell me why you suspect a Good Samaritan of sabotage? Seems to me the Tucker family would be indebted to Miss Lacewell, not looking to pin a crime on her. This only proves the opposite. I need solid evidence of intent to harm before I investigate an upstanding citizen like Lilith Lacewell."

"I don't have any solid evidence, Chief. That's what I'm after." Bradford twirled his hat. "On the hospital footage. Any indication of Miss Lacewell's presence at the hospital at the time of the incident."

Chief Nichols stared at Bradford in thoughtful silence, then said, "You were one of my best detectives, Bradford, and I've always felt you had the nose and instincts of a bloodhound. So, although there's no evidence to support your suspicions, I'm going to go with my gut and allow you in on the investigation."

Bradford slipped on his Stetson. "Thanks, Chief. You won't regret your decision."

"However," the chief began, and Bradford, halfway out of his seat, sank back down in the chair. I hovered over the computer screen to read the officer's report on Mama's run-in with the Devil's playmate.

"Detective Pressley won't be playing nursemaid.

I've given her this case, and I expect you to respect her position. You can teach her a lot, but I want her to take the lead. I'll dispatch Officer McMillian to the hospital when she comes in for her shift. She's my newest recruit and can use the experience. Pressley comes on duty at seven, and since there's little you can do at this hour, you can start then. Now, get out of here so I can get some shuteye. You might consider doing the same. You look jetlagged."

"Not a bad suggestion, Chief." Bradford stood and without a backward glance strode out of the chief's office and down the hall to the front desk.

"Thanks for all your help," he told Officer Middleton. "I'll be back at seven."

I followed him out of the station and to his car. Behind the wheel, he released a tired sigh. "The chief is right. It's time for a little shuteye." He fired up the engine and turned his rented sedan towards the farm, and I headed back to Dixieland Salon for a much needed R&R. Diamond's shift began in five hours, and I wanted to be fresh and alert when I joined their investigation into my attempted murder.

****

Some habitual lifestyle habits follow you into the afterlife. Like oversleeping. The morning sun casts long golden rays through the front plate glass window when I roused myself out of a zombie-like coma and wafted through the facial room door into the hallway. Since the shop was closed on Mondays, Scarlett and I had the place to ourselves. No worries of disturbing or frightening any clients and renewing the rumors of hauntings.

How ironic that I was now the haunter of my own

beauty shop.

I yawned several times and cast an envious eye at the kitchen door. My caffeine addiction had me hog-tied this morning, and I knew I shouldn't, but I willed myself present and made a pot of coffee. I had just finished my first cup when Scarlett drifted through the door. She frowned and folded her arms.

"I assume you have a reasonable explanation for your physical manifestation? Saint Peter warned you of the consequences of such actions. You may live to regret it."

"Shut up, Scarlett." I went over to the counter and poured another cup. "I have five minutes to feed the beast, and that's what I intend to do. Let me deal with the consequences. It is my body, you know, and I retain the right to choose."

"Aren't we grumpy this morning?"

I sat down at the table and cupped the warm mug with both hands. "I overslept," I said as an explanation for my moodiness. "And I'm tired of being a ghost—a shadow of my former self. I want my life back."

"I felt the same way when I woke up dead, but you're lucky. Heaven is giving you another chance at life."

"Yeah, and I'm grateful." I sipped down my second cup. Three minutes left. I poured another cup.

"I'd take it easy if I were you," Scarlett pointed out. "You're going to be bouncing off the walls with all that caffeine streaming through your bloodstream."

"In three minutes I'll be a ghost," I reasoned. "Give me three minutes, Scarlett. Three measly minutes of peace, while I finish my coffee, is all I ask. When I revert, you can resume your harassment."

"Deal," she said as she settled down across the table opposite me. "Now fill me in on your adventures with Detective Delectable."

I gave her a brief outline of last night's events. "I plan to tag along with them, Scarlett. I'm fairly certain Bradford will want to interview Lilith, and I want to hear what she has to say. I'd like you to come with us. For backup security. Man, you're awesome with a sword."

She beamed at me. "Let's hope the Powers That Be take note of my expertise. I'd like to move up the ranks until someday I might achieve the status of guardian angel to a new human entering the world. That's the highest position in Heaven, you know."

"No, I didn't. And I didn't realize you wanted to watch over a child."

"I never had the chance to be a mother. This is the next best thing."

"It's a hard, demanding job, but rewarding too. Geez, I'm sorry, and I sincerely hope you achieve your goal. You'd be a great guardian angel."

She was silent a moment, and then said, "Really? Do you honestly believe I am worthy?"

"I sincerely do, Scarlett." I gulped down the last of the coffee, placed the mug in the sink, and switched off the pot as I began to lose my solid form. "My time's up for now. Let's get moving, girlfriend. We have a ghost to bust."

Scarlett rolled her eyes. "Talk about corny, Jolene. You're unimaginative and unoriginal."

"And you're a phony with those store-bought boobs," I countered good-naturedly. "C'mon, let's track down Bradford and Diamond and join the investigation.

I have a feeling this situation is coming to a head."

"Wait, how's your arm and ankle? I'm good, but not that good."

I flexed my shoulders and ankle. "Doable."

Together we zoomed out of the salon and down to the police station to find Bradford and Diamond getting into an unmarked police cruiser.

"Let's hitch a ride in the backseat," Scarlett suggested. "There's a nip in the air this morning, and I'm cold. Please, I promise to keep quiet."

Her reasoning appealed to me, so we slipped into the backseat and waited as Bradford and Diamond buckled their seatbelts.

"Let's hope you're wrong about Lilith Lacewell," Diamond said. "I'd much rather think hospital negligence is to blame for Jolene's near-death than a competitor attempting murder. The security tapes I've viewed don't lead me to believe it was foul play. Although the tapes do confirm Miss Lacewell was in the hospital at the time of the incident, she was nowhere near ICU. I believe we're barking up the wrong tree, but I'm willing to look into every possible lead, Sam." She put the car into reverse and backed out of her assigned parking space.

"Head over to Lilith's shop," Bradford directed. "She should be there working with Roddy Hazard, the contractor. I'm sure she won't mind answering a few questions."

Diamond made a right onto Main Street. "How long are you stayin' in Whiskey Creek, Sam?"

"Until it's time to go."

"Still keeping matters close, I see."

"Only way to survive, Diamond, you know that. Or

you should know by now."

"I'm a slow learner, Sam. Always have been. Look how long it's taken me to make detective. And I wouldn't have without your help. I'd still be a patrol officer if you hadn't taken an interest in me."

"I know talent when I see it."

Diamond parallel-parked in front of Lilith's shop, Shear Indulgence. "I suppose you want to take the lead?"

Bradford nodded. "No, you start, and I'll jump in if necessary. You know what to do. I taught you well."

They both climbed out of the cruiser, and Scarlett and I wafted through the car to the sidewalk.

"Time for a little wake-up call for ole sulfur breath," I told her. "Keep your sword ready, Scarlett. Lilith doesn't play fair, so expect the unexpected. Plus watch out for her demon companions. They'll surely be lurking nearby."

"Do you think your plan will work?"

"What plan? I'm all out of ideas. I'm winging it."

From the sidewalk, I spotted Roddy's tall form through the plate glass window. He was perched high on a ladder installing retail shelving above what looked to be a reception desk. A couple of his crew were also clearly seen through the glass in various stages of construction.

Diamond rattled the doorknob. Locked. She rapped on the glass, and one of the men opened the door.

"Sorry, but the salon isn't open for business," he said. All work ceased as the men turned to look at the interruption.

Diamond flashed her badge. "That's okay, we're here on business. Is the owner in?"

Scarlett nudged me. "I'm going to scope out the back. You stay here with them."

I gave her an approving nod as I wafted over to Bradford's side. By this time Roddy had climbed down the ladder and stood in the opened doorway. He extended his hand to Bradford, and said, "Good to see you again, Sam. Billie Jo said you'd arrived. I'm sorry I haven't had time to look you up." He jerked his head toward the shop interior. "Work and all, you know." He turned to his crew. "It's okay, guys. Get back to work. I'll take care of this. Oh and Andy, see if Miss Lacewell is in the back room."

The men turned back to their task in progress, and immediately the noise of construction resumed. Roddy stepped back so they could enter. I wafted in behind them. "What's this about, Sam?" He hollered over the noise. "Jolene was still in serious condition this morning when Billie Jo called the hospital. Has something changed?"

Bradford shook his head and yelled over the racket. "She's holding her own. We're here on other business."

Lilith chose that moment to waltz out of the back room like Miss America in her victory walk after receiving the crown. Work halted, and all eyes fastened on her. Dressed in a form-fitting orange sweater dress and matching heels, she oozed sexuality and vivacity as she slinked toward us. Her amethyst eyes, alive and lusty, touched on Roddy, and then rested on Bradford. A slow, sensuous smile parted those full, tempting lips.

She moved closer to Bradford and offered her hand. "I can't imagine a nicer surprise than to see you again, Sam." Lilith's eyes caressed his tall form, and then settled on me with waves of cosmic radiation and contamination, but I didn't back down. I met her knowing gaze with determination and a silent challenge only we could discern.

Bradford slipped his Stetson from his head and took her hand. "I see you're getting ready for your grand opening." He dropped her hand and placed his hand on Roddy's shoulder. "Hazard's Construction is the best in town, Lilith, so I know you'll be pleased with his work. Roddy and his wife, Billie Jo, are good friends. However, Detective Pressley and I are here on official business. Do you suppose we could talk in private?"

Ever so slightly her phony expression shifted, and I tensed as the beast within grew angry and suspicious. Only those attuned to the spiritual world could sense the gathering force of darkness. The air crackled with tension until Diamond stepped forward and flashed her badge.

"I would appreciate your cooperation, Miss Lacewell. You can answer a few questions here or downtown. Here would be faster."

Lilith recovered in an instant and turned a fragile, distressed look at Roddy. His eyes glazed over, and his jaw clenched. Damn, my suspicions were correct. My brother-in-law was bewitched and well on his way to falling into Lilith's destructive trap, and I was helpless to prevent it.

"What's this about?" he burst out, his tone sharp with challenge. "You have no right to come in here and harass Lilith." His face flushed with vulnerability as he fought the unseen tentacles tightening around him and drawing him to Lilith's outstretched hand.

Bradford grabbed him. "Get a grip, man. What the

hell is the matter with you? Interfering with a police investigation? This isn't like you, Roddy. You've got a wife and family to think about." He jerked his head toward the front door. "You and your crew need to clear out of here until we're finished."

Roddy shook himself free of Bradford's grip. A muscle flicked at his jaw as he stared hard at Bradford. Tension cloaked the room, but Roddy jerked his head toward the door. "C'mon, guys, let's take a break." He started for the door but stopped and said over his shoulder, "We'll be back in half an hour, Miss Lacewell."

Worry congealed in my limbs as I watched Roddy and his crew exit the shop and climb into their work vehicles and drive off. The situation was grave, and unless someone stopped her, Lilith would destroy Billie Jo's family.

Diamond's rich, contralto voice interrupted my thoughts. "We only have a few questions for you, Miss Lacewell, concerning your relationship with Jolene Claiborne." She looked up from her notepad.

"Jolene and I had a strained relationship," Lilith responded in a stiff tone. "She didn't like me from our first introduction, but I feel certain jealousy is the root problem. I run into that a lot around older woman. Thankfully, the rest of the family didn't reflect her negative view. Especially after I saved Annie Mae from what could've been a nasty accident."

"Yes, I've read the report." Diamond made a notation on the notepad. "So, besides the one incident involving Annie Mae Tucker, can you recall any further confrontations between you and Miz Claiborne?"

"No, none that I can recall."

"A member of the family is certain Jolene suspected you of displaced interest in Roddy Hazard. Miz Claiborne expressed to this family member of your intentions to destroy the marriage and the man out of revenge. Is there any truth to that statement?"

She directed her answer to Bradford. "No truth whatsoever. I'm fond of Billie Jo, and I can't imagine why Jolene would tell such a lie."

Bradford remained quiet and allowed Diamond to continue her questioning.

"It's been confirmed by the hospital security tapes that you were in the hospital at the time of Miz Claiborne's incident with the ventilator."

"I was there." A quiver of a smile touched her lips.

"For what purpose?"

"I witnessed the shooting and wanted to express my support for the family. However, before I reached the ICU waiting room, I realized the family would be too distraught for visitors. I then promptly left the hospital."

"So you never made it to the second floor?" Diamond narrowed her eyes.

"Well, I'm sure you already know that I did." The smile widened. "And I'm sure the security tapes attested to me getting off the elevator and returning just after a few steps down the corridor from the waiting room. I'm sorry, Detective Pressley for wasting your time. I have no beef with Jolene. Now, if you don't have any further questions for me, I'll get back to work on my grand opening. Great seeing you again, Sam. Stop by later when you're alone so we can renew our acquaintance without an audience."

The words were meant for Bradford, but the

challenge was directed at me.

Chapter Nineteen
Twilight Time

"Lilith is launching her final assault tonight."

"Good work, Scarlett. Quick, give me the details."
We were in the backseat of Diamond's unmarked
cruiser on our way back to the police station. In the
front seat, Diamond and Bradford were discussing the
next logical step in the investigation since nothing had
come of Lilith's interview. Because you can't trap a
demon in the physical world, I knew they were facing a
dead end. I tuned them out so I could concentrate on
Scarlett's more important information.

"Well, while scoping out the back of the shop, I
stumbled upon two of Lilith's demon companions
fighting in the back alley. Before they could detect my
energy, I hid behind the big dumpster so I could
eavesdrop on their argument. Apparently, they were
fighting for the coveted position of second-in-command
on tonight's raid."

"Is the target still Roddy?"

"Yes, Lilith is confident he's receptive to her
invasion."

"I'm afraid she's right," I agreed. "I saw firsthand
his reaction to her when Diamond threatened to take her
downtown for questioning. He's bewitched, all right.
We have to stop her again."

"Easier said than done, Jolene. You're terrible with

a sword," she pointed out. "How do you propose we stall off her horde of demon companions? And not only are you a terrible swordfighter, but you're also a noisy klutz. Your words," she added at my frown. "Remember what Saint Peter said about Lilith being a dream weaver? We have to somehow catch her while she's vulnerable—which is, according to him—during Roddy's dream state. With all her energy focused on seduction, she'll be open to attack. We also must catch her unawares. If you're bumbling around waking the dead, how are we going to catch her unaware and stab her in the back? It must be timed perfectly for her to be vaporized."

I felt a burst of hopefulness. "To be honest, I don't have a clue how we're going to pull this off, but my senses are tingling off the charts with optimism. Don't you worry about me, I'll do my part. Last night taught me a few things. What else did you hear?"

"The ringleader will take his legion of demons and surround the house at sunset. The imps are out. Gone back to whence they came. Lilith sent for backup. The big, bad, kind and way out of my league. Lilith will arrive after Roddy is well into REM sleep. She also learned from last night's fiasco."

I thought for a moment. "Time-wise it would be best if we snuck into Billie Jo's house sometime in the midafternoon before Lilith's goons stake out the place. We can hide upstairs in the master bedroom. Lilith will never know we're there."

"If she finds us, we're toast."

"Have you a better plan? I'm open to suggestions."

"I've got nothing. Your plan it is. What now?"

I motioned to the front seat. "We ditch them and

head back to mission control and sketch out tonight's strategy for our attack."

"And a quick cat nap won't hurt," she added, stifling a yawn behind one hand. "I'm still bushed from last night. You had a massive shot of caffeine to boost your energy."

I smiled with remembrance. "Yep, that's the first thing I'm going to request when I wake up from this nightmare—a cup of strong, black coffee."

"I'd request sex if I were given a choice. Preferably a Scottish highland laddie—in a kilt. Oh, and minus the underwear."

Her dreamy smile made me laugh. "Good grief, Scarlett. You're a nymphomaniac. C'mon, we've work to do."

We shot through the car roof and zipped down Main to Love Avenue and through the salon's rear door. Scarlett immediately stretched out on the loveseat. "Wake me when it's time to go."

"Not so fast," I admonished. "We need to strategize."

"No, we don't. I'm a pantser. I fly by the seat of my pants." She closed her eyes.

"C'mon, Scarlett. Don't be a pain in mine."

No answer came from the loveseat. Seeing how I was getting nowhere with my ghost partner, I unsheathed my sword and practiced a few swashbuckling moves I'd learned from Hazell. As my sword swatted and whooshed through the air, Scarlett opened her eyes and said, "I can't sleep with all the noise you're making."

"If you won't help me plan, I figured I would practice my sword skills while you slept." I moved into the *En Garde* position. "Practice makes perfect they say."

She sat up with a thoughtful expression. "Actually that's not a bad idea. We could find a pasture or field out in the country and face off. With practice, we can synchronize our movements and strengthen our chances of victory. From there we can proceed directly to Billie Jo's house and take our positions."

I agreed with her plan, and we zipped out of town in the direction of my parent's farm where we would find open fields and pasturelands. Scarlett liked old man Durfree's berry farm, so we settled in a fallow backfield and squared off in mock battle scenarios.

It was a blast, and under Scarlett's tutelage I came out a much better sword fighter. Not great, but passable in an emergency. When the sun had progressed deep in the western sky, we sheathed our swords and raced back toward town. On the outskirts, we slowed down and approached the downtown historic district with caution in case any of Lilith's demonic warriors were scouting out the neighborhood in preparation for tonight's raid.

On the corner of Sixth Street, we decided it would be more practical to split up and do a little reconnaissance of our own, and meet up in the holly tree in Billie Jo's backyard. Scarlett would survey the back alleys of Sixth and Park, and I would probe the front streets for any sign of inhuman movement from the dark side.

Scarlett was perched in the highest branch when I settled down beside her. "Looks like we beat them here, Jolene. No sign of trouble. I scouted out the house and no one's home. Now would be a good time to check out the interior and find a good hiding place in the master bedroom before the family returns."

"It's too calm, don't you think?" I asked in nervous surprise. "Even the breeze has died down. Like the calm before the storm."

"Get a grip, Claiborne." A feral smile lit her eyes. "War is hell, and hell is war."

"Aren't you scared even a little?" I had to ask.

"Only of losing my place in Heaven," she answered. "Cleaning Saturn's rings isn't my idea of fun, and I have no intention of losing this battle. Gird your loins, Claiborne, and let's finish this job."

Her impromptu pep talk did little to boost my confidence, but I sucked it up and followed her to the roof of the house and down below. In the upstairs hallway, I ducked into Lynette's room and did a quick search. Clear. Back in the hallway, I continued my search until I met Scarlett in the master bedroom.

"The downstairs is clear of unclean spirits," she stated with a confident nod. "Everything okay on your end?"

I nodded. "Yeah, we've got the house to ourselves. Did you scout out a good hiding place?"

"The walk-in closet. There's a nice spot behind Roddy's golf clubs. You?"

I gazed around the room, seeing few options. "Under the bed is out. I could hide behind the drapes like I did that night in Richard Payne's library, remember?"

I was referring to our first murder investigation as a team. Scarlett's murder investigation, I might add. That's how she came to haunt Dixieland, but now's not the time to launch into that story, I still needed to find a great ambush spot.

"What about the bookcase?"

"Too tight. I'm thinking Billie Jo's antique wardrobe. It's large and has a clear view of the bed."

Scarlett floated over to one of the windows looking out over the backyard. "We can keep a lookout from here. You take the other window, and at the first sign of demonic activity, we can go into hiding."

I drifted over to the other window which offered a clear view of the side yard. "It won't be long now, it's close to sunset." I watched as a late model Dodge Charger came down the side street. "There's Billie Jo now. Roddy and Lynette won't be too far behind."

"And neither are Lilith's troops," Scarlett said. "They're settling into the trees and on the power lines now."

I scanned the tree line in the neighboring yards. Yep, dark shadows flittered among the still autumn leaves and evergreens. "We'll hold our positions until Roddy and Lynette make it home safely." The clanging of pots and pans drifted from downstairs. "Billie Jo is starting supper. Since Lilith won't make an appearance until Roddy is in bed, we have a short span of time to keep guard. He's in bed by nine."

Ten minutes passed before Lynette arrived home, and darkness had fallen by the time Roddy's pickup drove into sight and pulled around to the back alley. The back kitchen door opened and closed with a bang, and Roddy's hearty hello drifted upstairs.

Scarlett and I maintained our guard posts at the windows until they had eaten dinner and Roddy's boots sounded on the stairs. She flashed me a confident smile, and said, "I'll be watching from the closet, Jolene.

Remember to wait until Lilith is beyond the point of no return. Then we give it to her right between the shoulder blades."

I gave her a thumbs-up, and she disappeared through the closet door before I entered the wardrobe. Roddy entered the bedroom, and I heard the click of a lamp switch. The bathroom door closed and the shower came on. Several minutes passed before the shower stopped, and the bathroom door opened. Next, a drawer opened and then closed. Downstairs, Billie Jo and Lynette's murmured voices pinpointed their position in the kitchen as they cleaned the dinner dishes.

The bedclothes rustled when Roddy slipped into bed, and the lamp switch clicked off. His tired sigh rang loud as he wrangled his body into a comfortable position. As the room settled into quietness except for his gentle breathing, I cracked open the wardrobe doors and waited for Lilith to appear. And waited.

Lynette came upstairs, and then Billie Jo. She showered and changed into bedclothes and climbed into bed and released a tired sigh. From the wardrobe, I continued my vigil as her gentle snores joined Roddy's more vigorous snorts.

The moon had stretched its silvery beams far across the floor before I detected the slightest change in atmosphere. A slow chill began to invade the room along with a deep sense of evil, and I observed a dark shape lean over Roddy and inhale his man scent.

Lilith, in her seductive succubus form!

Fury almost choked me as she licked full, red lips, and floated her nude body over his and began to whisper erotic words into his ears. In his sleep, Roddy groaned and turned over onto his back. Billie Jo stirred but didn't awaken.

Watching Lilith's continued seduction dance with my brother-in-law made me feel like a demented voyeur, but I kept my tired eyes glued to the bed. To look away might cause me to miss the signal, and I could tell by Roddy's moans that it was drawing near.

I dared not make a sound when suddenly Roddy jerked his hips upwards, and a low, growl began deep in his throat. Lilith gasped, and I knew she had also reached the point of no return. Time for some good ole fashioned Southern justice! With my sword unsheathed and ablaze with righteousness, I flung open the wardrobe doors just as Scarlett emerged from the closet with sword blazing.

"Die, bitch," we screamed in union and plunged our flaming swords in the bulls-eye between her shoulder blades.

"Ahhh," Lilith screeched, her arms flailing to pull the impaled swords from her back. Red smoke poured from her wound. "Attack!" she wailed as she rolled off the bed and onto the floor, her black wings unfurled.

"Don't let her get away," Scarlett yelled at me and withdrew her sword to take another swipe as evil spirits swarmed the room like a black tide on a hot, Georgia seashore. She plunged into the swarm, battling the enemy with a steely vengeance.

I drew my sword, trying to concoct another plan. Whoosh, swords clashed, and sparks flew as I slashed and swung through a black mass, trying to reach Scarlett's side. My partner in battle was penned down by two huge demons. I shot to the ceiling and dove down like an avenging angel I'd seen on a TV show last month. My sword arched through the air and pierced the heart of a demon. He withered into a pile of black soot.

In the mayhem, Scarlett wiggled free, rolled onto her side, and leaped to her feet. She soared through the ceiling and back down in one long, sweeping arch that sent demons to the dust pile. Together with flaming swords, we faced a wounded Lilith, still sprawled crippled on the floor, those hypnotizing eyes glittering with raw hatred and fear.

"I ask for no quarter," she spat the words like poisonous darts and turned her back to us.

"And no mercy shall you receive," I replied. "Scarlett, let's finish this mission."

Scarlett gave me a quick nod. "I'm with you, girlfriend." She raised her sword, and together, in one perfectly timed lunge, we planted our swords deep into the gaping wound.

Lilith vaporized in a shower of red dust.

From the bed, Billie Jo sneezed. Roddy rolled over and gathered her into his embrace.

I sheathed my sword. "We're not needed here any longer. Let's leave them in peace."

"Well, Jolene, where do we go from here?" She gave me a questioning look.

"To the hospital where this whole damn thing started."

****

"Well done, ladies. Let me congratulate you on a job well done." Saint Pete beamed a triumphant smile from my hospital bedside. "I couldn't be happier with the results. The enemy has scattered, and Lilith is back in chains at the bottom of the great abyss. Fine job. Fine job."

Scarlett touched the hilt of her sword. "I guess you'll be wanting these back now?"

He cleared his throat. "Well, there is a matter of protocol I must adhere to, Scarlett. You should know the rules by now." He paused to scratch his chin. "However, because of your excellent leadership abilities and outstanding swordsmanship, and the fact your probation period is complete, the Powers That Be has decided to promote you into the Guardian Angel program." He snapped his fingers and Scarlett was clothed in a long, white gown complete with a golden sash and halo.

Scarlett gasped, and her cherry pink fingertips made a fluttering gesture. "Oh, thank you, sir. You won't be sorry. I'll make Heaven ring with applause." She tapped the floor with her shining white heeled slippers, then she hesitated the briefest moment before asking, "Is it possible to shorten the gown a mite? I might trip and fall in the line of duty."

He held up his hand in appeal. "Thanks are totally unnecessary, my dear. You've earned your place among the guardians. And no, you can't shorten the gown. Pants may be possible, but that will be decided by the Council. You'll begin your training period with Hazell and his staff where all the rules will be explained. We have an immediate position for you, but you must first earn your wings." He chuckled. "What is a guardian angel without her wings, I ask you?"

"Congratulations, Scarlett." I gave her a huge hug. "The child who lands you as his or her guardian angel is lucky indeed."

Saint Pete raised a bushy eyebrow. "Oh, it's not a child. Your guardian angel requested a transfer six months ago, and it was finally granted. As soon as Scarlett is ready, she'll be taking his place."

I mulled over his words. "I'm honored to be chosen as Scarlett's first assignment."

"Indeed." His kind smile widened. "But you weren't chosen. No one wanted the position. It goes to Scarlett by default."

Scarlett laughed. "I warned you this would happen someday, Jolene, but you didn't listen. Now we stuck together. I have the worse luck."

"That goes both ways, Scarlett," I pointed out with a mock frown. "I'm getting an angel with on-the-job training."

"Okay, enough about Scarlett," Saint Pete said with a stern tone. "I'd like to talk about you, Jolene, and what the Council of Noble Purposes has decided for your future." He snapped his fingers, and I was once again in the backless hospital gown. A shaft of cold air immediately had me grabbing the back of the gown and tugging it closed.

"As promised, you are being given a second chance." He wagged a finger under my nose. "But this time around use a little common sense. Stop and smell the roses, my dear, because, as I'm sure you've learned, life is short and full of surprises. The Council has plans for you, but I'm not at liberty to share them at this time. However, I will be popping in with updates. For now, trust the system and don't freak out if you find yourself with a new gift from above. Keep a cool head and deal with it until you learn how to use it. Okay, you two. Say your goodbyes. It's time for Scarlett and me to catch the long, black train back to Heaven, and you Jolene, back to your life in Whiskey Creek. We leave in three."

"Wait a minute," I protested. "You can't drop that kind of news in my lap and then scram back into the wide blue yonder. I need additional information. And who's watching my six while Scarlett's in training? And what about Mama? Is she back on the List?"

Saint Pete patted me on the cheek. "Your mother is off the List, for now, my dear. And as for who's watching your, ah, six, well, your Granny Tucker is filling in for now. Your grandfather is being assigned to Billie Jo's child. Now, if I've answered your questions satisfactorily, you may say your goodbyes."

I bobbed my head, and with one hand securely holding the back of my gown, I threw the other one around Scarlett. "Thanks for all your help. I couldn't have done it without you."

He snapped his fingers. "One."

"Or I you, girlfriend." She kissed my cheeks. "See you in a couple of weeks."

We both started laughing and crying. "Study hard, Scarlett. My ass is on the line," I said, scraping tears from my face with my free hand as Saint Pete threw me an admonishing glance. "I'll check on your gravesite while you're gone."

"Two."

Heaven's bright sunlight bathed the room in shades of silver and gold and shimmering opal as we stood facing one another. In life, we'd once been sworn enemies, but through the portal of death, we learned the value of lasting friendship and the wisdom of dedicated teamwork.

Her halo shimmered as bright as her smile. "Goodbye, Jolene. It's been fun."

"Not goodbye, Scarlett. See you later." I waved as

she began to fade.
    "Three."

Chapter Twenty
I've Got You under My Skin

I awoke to blinding light and the whirl and hum of life-sustaining machines. My senses told me that I had successfully returned to the land of the living although my mouth felt like sawdust, and my head pounded like a jackhammer on concrete. I had no idea how much time had elapsed since Saint Peter and Scarlett had departed, but it felt like years. I cracked open my eyes to see several nurses gathered around my bed, fiddling with beeping machines and tubes running out of my body.

A pretty blonde jerked back as her gaze met mine. She turned to another nurse. "Glory be, I don't believe it. Nancy, the patient is awake! Page Dr. O'Brien. Stat."

I watched the nurse scurry from the room, and a tall brunette joined the blonde at my bedside.

"Her stats are improving by the second," the brunette said with an approving nod. "Her heart rate and blood pressure have stabilized, and her oxygen levels are increasing. This is an amazing recovery. I didn't believe it possible. Her family will be so relieved with the news."

"God works in mysterious ways," the blonde said in an awed voice. "You're right. I wouldn't have believed it if I hadn't personally seen it happen."

I listened to the back and forth chatter of the nurses

with only half an ear. My mind kept replaying the past with crystal clear clarity, and I remembered everything that had been said and done on Earth and in Heaven.

Saint Pete with his blue suede shoes and handlebar mustache with the curled ends.

Lilith, the wind spirit. Defeated, and now chained in the great abyss.

Heaven, with its golden cobblestone streets and Southern rock music.

Samuel Bradford's return to Whiskey Creek.

And lastly, but not least, Scarlett Cantrell and her promotion to Guardian Angel. My soon-to-be guardian angel!

Peace and tranquility blanketed the room, and I felt supremely confident about the future. Mama was alive and well, and off the list of arriving saints. Deena was happily married to her prince, and Billie Jo glowed with health. For all intents and purposes, life was back to normal, and I could relax and concentrate on getting out of here and back to the salon.

A ripple of awareness brought me out of my musings, and I lifted my stunned gaze to see Saint Pete sail through the door in a white lab coat with a stethoscope draped around his neck. The two nurses stepped away from the bed, and he drew near. Dr. Peter O'Brien was embossed in cornflower blue on the lab coat.

He winked as he bent over me with his stethoscope in hand. "I hear you've made a remarkable recovery, my dear. Now, lie still while I examine you, and if all checks out, the nurses will remove the tube from your throat. I know you have a lot of questions for me and they'll be answered in due time."

My heart set up a steady thump, thump as his healing fingers moved over my physical body producing a tingling sensation from my toes to my eyelids, and I couldn't take my bemused gaze off him when he turned to the pretty blonde and said, "You may remove life support. She can breathe on her own." He returned his attention to me. "I'm going to speak with your family while the nurses remove the tubes and hindrances from you, but I'll be back to speak with you, understand?"

I nodded my confirmation and watched him scuttle away while the two nurses proceeded with the disconnections. The blonde injected something into my IV. "This will help with the pain," she said in a kind, soft voice.

My gag response triggered instantly when she eased the tube from my parched throat. I mimicked the action of drinking water, and she gave me a few sips from a cup. The relief was immediate, and I croaked, "Thank you."

After seeing to my comfort, both nurses left me alone with my thoughts. True to his word, Dr. O'Brien reappeared minutes later. He stood over my bed, tweaking his upturned mustache and studying me with a critical eye.

"Well, young lady, other than a small scar on your chest, you've come out of this latest adventure unscathed. I would say that you are an extremely lucky woman."

I touched the wound, and immediately felt the almost indistinguishable mark. Wow, that was some quick healing. "There are scars on the inside you can't see, but I'll survive."

"Of that, I have no doubt. You're a resourceful woman, Jolene Claiborne. You've been quite a surprise to the Powers That Be. Yes, indeed. Quite a surprise."

"Speaking of powers, how's Scarlett doing?"

He chuckled. "It's only been a week since she began training, but Scarlett is doing wonderfully. Hazell is taken with her."

"Do I smell romance?"

His bushy brows drew down over his merry green eyes. "I can't answer that question, but I can report that Scarlett is anxious to begin her duties as your guardian angel."

"When will that be?"

"All in due time, my dear." He broke off at the sound of voices. "My time is almost up, Jolene. That will be your family." He took my hand in his. "I won't see you again until the Council sends me with an assignment for you, but I'll be watching from above."

"Is that a threat?" I questioned with an affectionate smile.

"No, a warning." He released my hand and turned to leave. "Remember, Jolene, keep a cool head. Life is full of surprises," he tossed over his shoulder and walked out of the door.

With his exit, Mama and Daddy rushed in. Mama reached me first. "Jolene, we've all been so worried, but I knew you'd pull through. Didn't I say that, Harland?"

"Yes, Annie Mae, you surely did." Daddy drew up beside the bed and kissed my brow. "Glad you're back, honey. We missed you."

I squeezed both their hands. Tears pooled in my eyes. "I love you both so much."

"And we love you." Mama dashed away a stream of tears. "We only have a minute. The rest of the family is waiting for their turn to see you. Dr. O'Brien said you'd be moved out of ICU tomorrow morning so we'll see you then."

I kissed them both goodbye, and one by one, the rest of the family came in with well wishes for a speedy recovery. Becky and Jacob promised to bring Hannah by tomorrow to see me once I'd been moved to a private room and allowed young visitors. Deena and Ryder were the last. She erupted into tears upon entrance.

"Don't ever do that again, Jolene." She sobbed into a tissue. "My heart can't take it. I don't know what I'd do if I lost you…" she burst into tears again.

"You won't," I promised. "Atlanta isn't that far from Whiskey Creek. We can visit often."

Ryder placed a hand on Deena's shoulder. "We've decided not to relocate. My parents have decided they would be better moving into an assisted living facility. Deena and I can drive up twice a month to visit."

From my bed, I observed the love between them and experienced a profound joy at their happiness. At long last, Deena had received her happily-ever-after fairy tale ending with a great guy. No one deserved it more than her.

A nurse stepped into the room with a fresh IV bag. "She's had enough visitors for now. You can visit again tomorrow."

We said our goodbyes, and I settled down for a long night. After being in a comatose state, my body ached with restlessness, and I wanted nothing more than a long walk in the peaceful countryside with the comforting sounds of nature.

Preston walked in my room instead.

"I came as soon as I could get away," he said, kissing my forehead, before pulling up a chair alongside the bed. "The hospital is all abuzz with our miracle patient. I've been bragging about my wondrous girlfriend's strength and stubbornness."

I adjusted my smile to match my mood. "About that," I began in a serious tone. "I'm afraid you're going to have to find someone else to fill that position, Preston."

"It's the guy with the silver badge, isn't it?" He tried to sound casual.

"Yes, the cop gets the girl."

He stood. "I hope he appreciates his good fortune."

"He doesn't know how lucky he is yet."

"You haven't told him?"

I swept my hand down the length of my prone body. "I've been kinda laid up in case you haven't noticed."

He chuckled. "Tell the lucky cowboy he won, Jolene, before he rides off into the sunset with another woman." He pecked my cheek. "A kiss to remember you by. I don't mind admitting that I'm going to miss you."

"Am I interrupting?" Bradford's husky voice sounded over Preston's shoulder. "The nurse said I could stop in for only a minute, but I can leave if you wish."

"Tell him," Preston whispered into my ear, then turned around to address Bradford. "No, you're not interrupting and congratulations."

"For what?" Bradford shook Preston's outstretched

hand.

Preston didn't answer, just chuckled softly and left the room.

Bradford slipped his Stetson from his head, drew close and planted a tender kiss on my lips. "I'm so glad to see you awake, Claiborne. You scared the life out of this ole cowboy." He hitched the chair closer to the bed and sat down. "How are you feeling?"

A rush of emotions goosed me as his eyes blazed into mine. It was all happening so fast. The moment I'd been longing for had finally arrived. Here was my second chance at life, at love, and all I could do was clutch the bedsheets with my shaking hands and smile like an idiot. Why was it so hard to say *I love you* to the greatest guy on the planet?

"Pretty good considering I was gunned down at my sister's wedding," I managed to croak out.

"You'll be happy to know we caught the guy."

"It's good to know justice will be served."

"I'm staying out at the farm. Your family has been most gracious hosts, but I'll be leaving in a couple of days. That is, as soon as you're out of here and back home."

His announcement left me reeling, and I responded without thinking. "Will you marry me?" I felt like a lightning bolt had hit me when I said the words. Surprised by my own actions, I stared at him, dazed and incredulous, and slightly nauseated. My face flamed at his expression and the silence stretching uncomfortably between us.

"Take it back, Jolene," he finally said in a gentle tone. "Now is not the time for emotional outbursts."

I took a deep, long breath and considered my next

move. Bradford had given me an easy out. Just take it back, he'd said. Easy to do, but I was done with taking the easy way out. No, I was ready to jump into life and take a risk with the man I loved.

"Marry me," I repeated without hesitancy.

He shook his head. "This is kind of sudden, don't you think?"

"I want to wake up with you on snow-capped mountains," I repeated a phrase he'd written on one of the floral arrangement cards. White roses.

"You hate the snow."

"Walk with me in wide open spaces." Another phrase. The Asters.

He cracked a smile. "In those stilettoes? I can't afford you."

I saved the best for last, and I placed my hand in his. "With me, every day will be an adventure." The Carnations this time.

He bent over the bed to brush my lips with his. "I guess there's only one thing left to say after that heartfelt proposal. Yes, Jolene, I'll marry you, and carry you away to snow-capped mountains. I'll walk with you in wide open spaces, and every day will be an adventure."

The tall brunette nurse interrupted us, and we shared our good news with her. Delighted, she gave us an additional five minutes of together time, and then backed out of the room with smiles and congratulations.

"Are you sure about this, Jolene?" Bradford asked. "It'll mean leaving everything and everyone behind in Whiskey Creek, and I know how much you hate change."

"Yes, I do hate change," I admitted with a wry

smile. "But I've learned that life is short and full of surprises, and when you least expect it, life's path can lead you down some fascinating detours."

"What about the salon?" He eyed me uneasily.

"I can't answer that question," I said with a twinge of sadness. "Deena and Billie Jo both have a lot going on in their lives. There's a good chance the salon will close. But I haven't left yet."

He frowned at my answer. "You're not backing out of your own proposal, are you?"

I glanced over his shoulder at the faint outline of the glistening sword of light resting against the corner wall where I had placed it earlier, and the thrill of another adventure washed over me. Saint Pete had voiced the Council's future plans for me. Where and when I could only guess. Wyoming? Whiskey Creek? Other destinations beyond my imagination? I didn't know much, but I did know Sam Bradford was in for the biggest change of all if he married me. Yes, if he married me, once I shared my latest escapade with him. You see, if we stepped onto the path of matrimony, him and me and Scarlett would become partners with Heaven's forces, and Sam wasn't fond of my invisible world. Our future would be determined with the telling of my tale.

I squeezed his hand, and said, "Brace yourself, Sam, I have something to tell you."

"I'm not going to like this, am I?" Concern deepened his voice.

"Probably not," I answered. "But keep an open mind and don't interrupt until I'm finished."

He nodded, and I told him everything starting with Lilith's arrival in the facial room and ending with Saint

Pete's announcement regarding Heaven's future plan for me. When I sputtered to an end, his face was blank with astonishment. He pushed himself out of the chair and paced the hospital room, stopping every few steps to glance over at me in consternation. After several minutes of silent pacing, he seemed to have reached a decision and collapsed back into the chair. He clutched my hand in his and took a deep breath. "I can't say that I'm happy about living in a paranormal world, Jolene, but I've asked you to change your world for mine. I can do no less for you. I love you, Jolene, and we'll figure this out together."

"Your life will never be the same," I pointed out.

He arched a brow. "My life has been insane since I met you. What's a little more insanity when I get you for a lifetime?"

"Scarlett will be permanently attached to my side," I warned.

"I can handle Scarlett," he boasted with a chuckle. "What I can't handle is enduring a wedding on the scale of Deena's. Please tell me you want a small affair."

"We could elope," I suggested.

"That's agreeable with me. What did you have in mind?"

"Vegas."

He grinned. "Sin City? What will Saint Pete say?"

"That I'm incorrigible." I giggled. "And he would be right, too."

"So Vegas, it is. Anything else?"

I squeezed his hand. "Yeah, I want the whole Elvis experience."

"What about your family? They'll insist on sharing our happiness."

"I'm sure they'll understand if we keep our special day to ourselves," I said. "Besides, Ryder and Deena have a honeymoon to enjoy, and Billie Jo and Roddy have a family to see after. But whatever the future brings, I'm confident Heaven is on our side. Who knows what tomorrow may bring?"

Outside the hospital window, a streak of light flashed in the night sky, and even with my limited view from the bed, I could've sworn I glimpsed a legion of angels whizz by. Was it possible Saint Peter had given his blessing? I hoped so, for I was embarking on the most thrilling adventure imaginable.

Not ready to give up your Jolene and Scarlett fix?
Then check out the first few pages of…

Jingle Bells and Krampus Spells

A Scarlett Cantrell Christmas Novella

Chapter One
Blue Christmas

I seized the opportunity with gusto. Hazell shifted those glorious baby blues off me for one millisecond, and I arched my glittering sword of light high above my head and swung with all my kick-ass feminine might. My attack caught him by surprise, and his sword dislodged from his firm grip and tumbled to the ground where it stretched out on the grass like a lazy silver python taking a long summer nap.

"I win." I breathed in the sweet scent of victory. My first of many to come, I hoped.

My fencing instructor gave a crooked grin. "You had an unfair advantage, Scarlett. I warned you several times, and you have ignored my concerns regarding your choice of wardrobe. I was distracted."

I sheathed my sword and delivered a catty smile. "A guardian angel must be prepared for the unexpected. Your words," I added at his frown. "And, in my defense, I'm clothed in the approved apprenticeship uniform. It just happens to be a mite tight, that's all."

The blond giant towered over me, his brilliant eyes shining with mirth, and a forbidden thrill shot through my veins, and for the thousandth time since my death, I hungered for life and the pleasures it promised. Call me sinful, but I hadn't mastered my desire for the virtuous Hazell. He reminded me of one of those hunky Viking lords displayed on the covers of romance novels so trendy on Earth right now. Long, flowing locks of golden hair, sizzling eyes of righteous purpose, and yummy buns of steel.

Deena had those type of books sprinkled all over her office at Dixieland Salon. I had salivated over them until I'd met Hazell. In my eyes, he was the embodiment of masculinity. Lose the wings and virtuous nature, and boy-oh-boy what I could do with him. But it would not happen no matter how much I fantasized. We were celestial citizens of the Heavenly sort. He, an Archangel in the Order of the Guardsmen, and I, a Southern girl trying to earn her angel wings.

An unlikely pair. Mismatched, one might say.

Saint Peter would definitely say. Not the romantic type, Saint Peter. A lover of rules. He'd blow a gasket if he knew I'd snatched a kiss from the hunky Hazell out behind the white marble headquarters of the Council of Noble Purposes. A stolen kiss had kick-started my fascination for the big guy with the massive wings.

Yep, a forbidden secret, for sure. Guardian angels are forbidden to fall in love.

"Scarlett, did you hear me?" Hazell's voice broke through my thoughts. "You're doing excellent. Your sword-fighting skills are above average, and I'm happy to report you're ready for the next phase in your training. I know you're eager to take your position as a guardian angel."

"Jolene can wait," I protested, not willing to leave the comfort of Heaven—or Hazell. The thought of being separated from him turned my stomach. "You're right about me." I waved a hand down my curvy body, pausing over my oversized boobs. "I have a way with males, and I use it to my unfair advantage." I shook my bronze ponytail. "I have a reputation for not playing fair."

Hazell's piercing gaze swept over me, melting my knees. "You will be fine, Scarlett. You must take your place among the guardians. It's what you've been working toward."

He was right. I had worked hard to accomplish my goal to become a guardian angel—which is one of the highest achievements in Heaven for a departed soul. But somewhere along the way, I had lost sight of Earth. And Jolene. Rumor around Heaven was she and Sam had eloped to Vegas and now experienced their HEA in Jackson Hole, Wyoming. Good for her, bad for me, because I'd changed my mind about leaving Heaven to become her guardian angel.

Luminescent dashes of golden light shimmered from the radiant cosmic love surrounding us, and I could faintly make out the voices of the Hallelujah Choir coming from the Golden City just over the Galaxy Mountains. Heaven is like that. Shiny and warm and filled with happy celestial citizens and animals.

The flutter of angel wings brought a visitor to the training center on the outskirts of the city. I groaned when I recognized Cooper, one of Saint Peter's messenger boys, settle down from the up drift he'd rode in on. He folded his wings and strode over to where Hazell and I were standing. He gave a nod of acknowledgment to Hazell, then addressed me with his usual stone-faced manner. "Your immediate presence is required."

Cooper never wasted words or smiles. To the point without fuss. His dress code reflected his straight and narrow personality. A three piece pin-striped gray suit. Black loafers. Wire-rimmed glasses. Short cropped brown hair.

I gave a mock salute. "Message received, over and out. Reporting to headquarters in ten."

His unamused gaze swept over me. "The Boss is waiting." His brow lifted in a challenge. "Now."

Our gazes clashed. Twerp. Did he believe an errand boy in a business suit could intimidate me? One of the mighty Guardians of the Heavenly Realm? Ha. Not in a million years. Excitement corroded my thinking. My grip tightened on my sheathed sword, and I took a step backward to prepare for battle. The sword hummed to life as I withdrew it, and I squealed in surprise when a persuasive grip closed over my wrist.

"You must learn to corral your rebel blood, Scarlett," Hazell instructed, even though his mouth quirked with humor. "A warrior only uses her might to protect her charge. Not to dissect another angel, and certainly not one of Saint Peter's staff. Be ever mindful of the power you yield."

Hazell's gentle reminder did the trick. Cooper dropped his superior attitude, and my breath expelled in a shaky whoosh. I sheathed my fiery sword, and muttered a hasty "Thank you," under my breath.

Reprimanded for my inappropriate behavior, I softened my expression and turned to Cooper. "A thousand pardons to you, sir. I will report to my superior when I finish my lesson."

"Well, then, I will take my leave," Cooper huffed out in a polite but patronizing voice, and it took all my reserve not to carve him up like a Thanksgiving turkey. Hazell cleared his throat, and I relaxed my stance.

Saint Peter's angel caught the next breeze, and just before he scooted behind a fluffy white cloud, I heard his nasal voice urging me "Not to dawdle." To my determent, I shot him a bird and earned another reprimand from Hazell.

"Scarlett, you must learn to control your human passions," his gentle voice urged. "They will lead you astray if you can't manage them."

Speaking of passion. Hmmm. I wonder.

I trailed a finger along his arm. "Hazell, before I go," I kept my voice low and seductive, "I have a parting gift from a grateful student."

"The Council frowns on gift-giving between students and instructors."

"I don't kiss and tell."

"It's forbidden."

"Forbidden is the spice of life."

His brows flickered. "Not for angels, Scarlett. We aim high and are above reproach. Never forget your training and how hard you've worked to get here. Not all human spirits are chosen to serve in the Guard. Be honorable and stay out of trouble."

I sighed and dropped my hands to my side, once again humbled and reminded of my new standing in the Golden City. The mighty Archangel Hazell urged me to stay out of trouble. Good advice for angels, but I wasn't a full-fledged angel yet. My natural human rebellion reared its ugly head at the most inopportune times. Not that I wished to sin, it just happened.

"I promise to make you proud, Hazell." My voice quivered with forbidden emotion.

His voice softened. "Don't bend the rules, Scarlett, and you'll do fine."

Infused with Heaven's perfection, I touched the sword at my side, crossed my fingers for good luck and caught the next up-drift for the Golden City and my meeting with Saint Peter.

Penny Burwell Ewing

A word about the author…

Penny Burwell Ewing was born and raised in Fort Pierce, Florida. Growing up in a Southern coastal town gave her the best of small town living where the residents look out for one another. Her interest in writing began in the 1970s when she consumed every bodice-ripper published and decided to try her hand at entertaining herself. It worked and she is now working on her sixth novel. Once a professional Cosmetologist, Penny draws on her humorous experiences behind the chair to add spice to her Haunted Salon series. She now resides in Tifton, Georgia. Her favorite pastime is counted cross stitch and fine needlework.

Thank you for purchasing
this publication of The Wild Rose Press, Inc.

For questions or more information
contact us at
info@thewildrosepress.com.

The Wild Rose Press, Inc.
www.thewildrosepress.com

To visit with authors of
The Wild Rose Press, Inc.
join our yahoo loop at
http://groups.yahoo.com/group/thewildrosepress/